HER HEARTLESS KING

ELLA JADE

Her Heartless King© 2022 Ella Jade

Editor: Zero Alchemy

Cover Designer: Dark City Designs

Photographer: Eric Battershell

Cover Model: Johnny Kane

All rights reserved under the International and Pan-American Copyright Conventions. No part of this book may be reproduced or transmitted in any form or by any means, electronic or mechanical, including photocopying, recording, or by any information storage and retrieval system, without permission in writing from the publisher.

This is a work of fiction. Names, places, characters and incidents are either the product of the author's imagination or are used fictitiously, and any resemblance to any actual persons, living or dead, organizations, events or locales is entirely coincidental.

Warning: the unauthorized reproduction or distribution of this copyrighted work is illegal. Criminal copyright infringement, including infringement without monetary gain, is investigated by the FBI and is punishable by up to 5 years in prison and a fine of $250,000.

http://authorellajade.com/

 Created with Vellum

CHAPTER 1

Luciana

"Now you are my prisoner, my little butterfly."

Romero's words played in my mind like a horrible nightmare that I couldn't wake up from. They were the last words I heard before I drifted off into a fitful night of sleep, and the first account I woke up to in the morning. A constant reminder that there was no escaping him. No running from this life.

I hadn't seen him in two days. Not since the night he confronted me and told me he knew I was a traitor. He left the house and hadn't returned. I didn't dare try to leave. There were too many guards surrounding the property. Even if I managed to escape, where would I go?

If I went back to my family, I'd have to tell them I failed at this mission and Romero knew what I was up to. If I did that, my husband would make good on his promise and kill one of them. No matter how awful my uncle was, I wouldn't have his blood or any other on my hands. I wasn't like any of them. I would never understand how this life could intrigue them or why they would choose to be the way they were.

They may own me, but I would try to control what I could. I had to hope there was a way to get myself out of this mess. For now, I'd bide my time and do what my husband told me to do. Being stuck between the man they forced me to marry and the people I reluctantly called my family wasn't the best position to be in, but I would find my way out.

"Lu," a calming voice said from behind me.

I was aware that Gio had been in the house these past two days, but he had left me alone until now. His presence was strangely comforting, even if he didn't interact with me. I set the book I wasn't really reading on the coffee table and turned to face him as he entered the sunroom.

"What's up?" I asked.

"I wanted to check in with you." He sat next to me. "You've been scarce these last couple of days."

"I'm staying out of your way." I glanced out at the backyard as one of the men was doing a perimeter check. "I'm sure you're as upset with me as your brother is."

"He might have more of a reason to be upset

with you, but I will say it surprised me when I discovered what you were doing."

"I didn't ask for any of this." I leaned my head against the back of the sofa, fighting off the physical and emotional exhaustion that had plagued me since I moved into this house. "I never wanted to hurt him. I didn't want to be caught in the middle. My family trapped me."

"I'll always have my brother's back, but I can understand where you're coming from."

"You can?"

"Your family put you in a difficult position. I get you couldn't say no." He reached for my hand. "But you came after Romero and you put us in danger. It's going to take him a lot longer to forgive you."

"I didn't know how to stop it."

"You could have told him."

"Would he have reacted any better if I had told him sooner?"

He ran his thumb along the bruises on my wrist and then glanced at my neck. Romero's firm grip had left marks on my flesh.

"His anger gets the best of him," he said.

"I'm fine." I pulled my hand away and tugged on my sleeve to cover my wrist. "Things got heated between us. I hurt him and he didn't know how to handle that. He reacted the way you would have expected him to."

"He doesn't want to be abusive."

"Like your father?"

"He told you about that?" Gio seemed surprised. "He doesn't like to talk about that. If he opened up to you about our parents, he must really like you."

"That was before." We connected on a level I never thought possible. If we had come together under different circumstances, we might have worked, but now there was no reason to think about a future with Romero. I was in survival mode.

"If he put his hands on you in anger, he felt desperate, like you backed him into a corner. I'm not excusing his behavior, but when he found out about your deception, he snapped."

"There's no doubt in my mind he wanted to kill me." The murderous look in Romero's eyes when he told me he knew I had deceived him was something I would never forget. Why didn't he kill me? Would I ever understand his reason for sparing me.

"I'm glad he didn't kill you."

"So am I, but that's probably not off the table for him." This screwed up life of mine got crazier by the day, "He hasn't been home since he found out. I don't know what it will be like when he comes back. What if we can't live together?"

"If he wanted you gone, you would be already. You're going to have to give him time. It's going to take a while for you to earn back his trust."

"Do you think that's even possible?"

"It'll be a hard sell. I mean, no one has ever done it, but I have a feeling you might."

Did I want to?

"As twisted as your relationship seems now, my brother cares about you. If he didn't, he wouldn't have cared that you were here to help your family. If your betrayal didn't hurt him, he would have killed you. I've seen him kill for less."

"Should that flatter me?"

"Was it all an act for you?" Gio asked. "Was any part of your marriage real?"

"Yes." That was what made this all so difficult. "More than I ever thought possible. I didn't want to marry him, but when I did, something changed. As brutal and terrifying as he is, I saw another side of him. One that I fell for. One that I wanted to protect, but I didn't know how."

"Maybe you should tell him that."

"Why are you rooting for me?"

"As vicious as you think my brother is, you should have seen him before he married you."

"He was worse?" That was troubling.

"You're changing him, Lu," Gio said. "I don't know if that's a good thing or a bad thing. It's probably bad for business, but he's needed you in his life for a long time."

"It's too late now." I fought back the tears that needed to wait until I was alone. "Whatever we were building is ruined. My family made sure of that.

When they promised me to Romero, they knew we could never make it. I've always been expendable to them."

"You can still salvage this."

"How?"

"Do what Romero asks of you."

"Go against my family?"

"You just said you mean nothing to them. Turn the tables on them. Make them pay for how they treated you, and in the process, you'll gain Romero's trust. It will take time, but it can be done."

"What if I don't want any of this?"

"Are you saying my brother isn't worth the fight?"

"I'm saying even if I do what he asks of me, what guarantee do I have that he'll want anything to do with me after? Once I betray my family, I'll never be able to go back to them." That wasn't such a bad thing, if they didn't kill me. "If Romero can't forgive me, what then?"

"You don't have the luxury of controlling any of this. They put you in a shitty situation, but I can promise you, Romero is a way out. Take it."

"By doing exactly what he says, even if it could get me killed."

"You're safer with him than anywhere else. Despite what he says, he'll protect you. I know my brother. I know what he's capable of and what he isn't."

My body tensed when the front door opened and

then slammed shut. I hopped to my feet, deciding if I had time to make it to the back staircase and upstairs before Romero spotted me.

"Don't run away," Gio said. "Face him, stand up to him, and earn his respect."

"I can't."

Romero's fast footsteps pounded against the hardwood floor, getting closer with each frantic breath I drew. What if he had changed his mind and decided to come back here and end my life? I headed toward the kitchen, but it was too late.

"Don't leave on my account." Romero leaned against the archway of the sunroom. "Not when we have so much to discuss."

"Where have you been?" I asked.

"Were you worried about me? Afraid one of your family members took me out?" He smiled at Gio. "You wouldn't let that happen, would you?"

"You know I wouldn't," Gio responded.

"That's because you're loyal and always have my back," Romero said. "I can't say that about everyone around here."

Obviously, he was still upset about what my family forced me to do. There was no use in defending myself or apologizing. He wasn't in a forgiving mood and I didn't have any excuses. I betrayed him and now I had to pay the price.

"Why don't we go to your study and discuss some

things?" Gio pointed to the hallway. "I have a few papers that need signing."

"Not now." The emotionless void in Romero's eyes worried me. "I want to be alone with my wife."

Please don't leave me, Gio.

CHAPTER 2

Romero

Gio shook his head in disapproval, but honored my request and left me alone with Luciana. She turned away from me and gazed out at the backyard. She rocked back and forth and fidgeted with her hands. At least she was smart enough to be afraid of me after what she had done.

After almost strangling her the other night, I realized I needed to put some space between us. My goal was not to kill her. I just wanted to make her understand no one betrayed me. I needed to leave and calm down, so I went to my penthouse and thought this whole situation through. I couldn't say that I resolved anything in my mind, but I couldn't stay away forever.

When I stood behind her, she straightened her posture and tensed. I clenched my fist at my side. Why did it bother me that she was so uncomfortable around me? I've seen her with Gio, and Jag, and the other guys around the house. She doesn't shy away from them. She was kind and polite. They made her laugh. I could be harsh and mean. We got off on the wrong foot, but we were communicating and working through that, and then... *fuck!* Every time I thought about her deception, It filled me with rage. I could never be the man she needed if every other thought in my head made me want to kill her.

"What have you been up to while I was gone?" I stepped closer to her, placing my hands on her arms. "Behaving?"

"I haven't spoken to anyone in my family since you left."

"Good."

"You didn't tell me where you went."

"I don't answer to you." I squeezed her arms. "It's the other way around."

"Why am I here?"

"You know why."

I spun her to face me, hoping to get a glimpse of her beautiful eyes, but as I expected, she dropped her gaze. When I saw the bruises on her neck, I silently cursed myself for losing it the way I had. No matter how much she deserved my anger, I shouldn't have put my hands on her. I tried hard to push back the beast but I failed. My father would be proud.

"You're going to help me get the revenge I seek on your family."

"Revenge for sending me here and spying on you?"

"As much as I'd like for them to know I caught you and I'm making you pay, that's not the only act I need to avenge."

"I don't want to be caught in the middle of this." She tried to wiggle out of my hold, but I wrapped my hand around her waist and tugged her to me.

"Do you want to know why your family wanted the location of my safe house?"

When our eyes connected, hers widened.

"That's right. I know all your transgressions. Every detail you relayed about my personal business is all up here." I tapped my forehead. "A constant reminder of who I married."

She looked away from me again.

"Your uncle wanted the location of my safe house because someone in your family killed a loyal employee of mine to send a message. They dumped his badly mangled body on the back porch to show me they could get to me. Now that house is useless to me."

"I'm sorry," she whispered.

"His name was Arturo." I pulled her against me, trying to get her to look up, but she didn't oblige. "He had a seven-year-old daughter, and he adored his mother. Do you know the work the undertaker had to perform just so that his mother could say goodbye?"

She shook her head.

"After they killed him, they must have put him in water for a few days. I don't have all the details, but do you have any idea what happens to your body after you've been soaking in water for days? How horrible it is? We could Google it and get some perspective."

"Please stop it."

"Why? You don't like that after all Arturo had gone through, you're responsible for giving them a location for dumping his body? What your treachery caused? You helped them with the lack of respect they showed him."

"I didn't know why they wanted the address."

"What they did to my guy will not go unanswered."

"I don't want to be part of anymore death or violence."

"Do you think you have a choice?" I laughed before pushing her over to the sofa and making her sit. "I should kill one of your cousins in retaliation. That would certainly throw your uncle off balance and leave his territory ripe for the taking."

"No." She raised her voice. "You said if I did what you wanted, you wouldn't hurt any of them."

I couldn't kill any of the Torrios without permission from the higher families. If I did, it would cause an all-out war. One I wasn't prepared for. Luciana didn't need to know that. For now, I would use the threat of killing her family as leverage. Was that wrong? Absolutely. But what she had done to me was much worse.

"As long as you know your role." I sat down next to her. "I have your first assignment."

I couldn't start a war over Arturo, but if I was patient, the Torrios would get what they deserved. I would make sure of that. I'd bring them all down and make Luciana watch.

"I'll have something for you to give your family soon." I traced my finger along her jaw. "All you have to do is feed it to them."

"Please. Romero." She twisted her body toward me. "Can't you forget this feud and walk away?"

"No." I ran my thumb along her trembling bottom lip. "Where would the fun in that be?" I inched closer to her, cornering her between me and the arm of the sofa. "You want me to forgive you, don't you?"

She didn't say anything when I swiped my lips along hers.

"The only way that can happen is if you do what I say."

"You're never going to forgive me."

"Never is such a long time." I dropped my hand between her legs. I couldn't kill her, but I could make her suffer in other ways.

She sucked in a breath when I moved my hand over her pants.

"Are you wet for me?" With my free hand, I yanked her hair, pressing her lips to mine and kissing her hard on the mouth. She gasped when I released her. "It's been a few days since I fucked you."

She squeezed her legs shut.

"You don't want me to touch you?" I removed my hand and undid my belt. "Then you can touch me." I unbuttoned my pants and lowered my zipper. "You need to learn your place. There is no reason I should suffer for your indiscretions. You're my wife and you will act like it."

I grabbed her hand and shoved it down my pants, running it over my hard shaft.

I thought she might deny my request, but to my surprise, she wrapped her delicate fingers around my cock and got to work. I rested my head against the back of the sofa as she relieved the stress of the past few days. I breathed in the scent of her peppermint shampoo, fighting back the urge to pull her into me and bury my face in her wild curls. I couldn't allow myself to fall any deeper for her. Whatever had developed between us was over. From now on, it was business and sex.

"That's it, baby." I flexed my hips forward, moving in time with her hand. "Make me come."

When she brought her lips to mine, I turned my head. I didn't want intimacy. I didn't want her gentle, caring touch. I closed my eyes so I couldn't see the hurt in hers. What did she want from me?

I twisted my fingers in her hair, keeping her lips away from mine. She took her frustration out on my cock, jerking me off at a fierce pace. The familiar ache developed inside my balls, intensifying with each of her aggressive tugs. *That's my girl!*

I quickly guided her head between my legs. She glanced up at me as she opened her mouth, allowing me to shove my cock inside. I gripped her hair and moved her forward until my balls hit her chin.

"Fuck!" Her hot mouth drove me to insanity. "I'm going to come."

She held still, letting me take control. With a couple swift thrusts forward, I shot my seed down her throat. She released me from between her lips and swallowed what I'd given her.

She got up on her knees, caressing my thigh with her hand. I wanted more than anything to fuck her, but that wasn't our arrangement. If she wanted my dick buried inside her, she had to work for it.

"That was fantastic." I ran my thumb along her wet lips. "There's a file in the guest bedroom. Read it and tell Vincent about it. He'll know what to do with it."

"Romero."

"It's the only way now." I adjusted my pants and stood from the couch. "Do what I ask and I'll reward you." I cupped her chin in my hand, holding her face between my fingers. "You're out of options. I'm all you got."

She let out a frustrated breath as I released her from my unyielding hold and I walked down the hall. When I married her, I thought I could stop being the animal that I was before her. I allowed her to change me. As I entered my study, I clenched my fists. I had never let anyone into my home, into my heart, and look how that fucking turned out. I should have trusted my instincts. I should have known I wasn't meant for love and flowers, and all that other sweet bullshit.

I poured myself a drink, picked up the file on my desk, and took a seat. That blowjob should have taken the edge off, but all it did was make me crave her more. I wanted more than anything to sink into that tight pussy of hers. To claim her and make sure she knew who owned her.

Later.

I opened the file and studied the pictures of Luciana's parents. This was no car accident. Someone covered up these murders. Who? What was the motive?

Why did this bother me so much?

CHAPTER 3

Luciana

I stormed up the steps and into the guest bedroom. Why did I allow Romero to get to me? I had to give him what he wanted without feeling, without wanting, without desiring.

I closed my eyes and tried to settle down from our encounter in the sunroom. He terrified me to the point of arousal. How was that even possible? Was there something wrong with me? What kind of woman craves a man who threatens her life? *Me.*

I flipped through the file Romero left on the dresser. I paced the room, debating on what I wanted to tell Vincent. Would this information Romero wanted me to give him end up getting one of my cousins killed?

None of this was my fault. My family put me in this position when they married me off to a frightening arms dealer. They shoved me in the middle of their business. A business I knew nothing about, and now I was paying a high price for a life I didn't want anything to do with.

I composed a quick text to Vincent with unsteady fingers.

I have something for you.

I looked over the file. It listed locations and names of people I had never heard of. My phoned dinged with his reply.

Let's discuss in person.

His response didn't surprise me, but did it matter how we communicated? Romero figured out the truth no matter how careful we'd been.

I'll come see you this week.

Good girl.

I sat on the edge of the bed and scrolled through my phone, looking at schools I'd researched. All I had to do was finish my bachelor's degree and then I could start law school. Maybe by the time I was ready to do that, I would be free of this stupid mess. There were some intriguing choices across the country. Maybe even out of the country. I would change my name. No more Torrio, no more Bilotti. I could be free.

A girl could dream.

The sad part of this whole situation was I could still see myself in a relationship with Romero. Not as a mafia wife. Not as someone who could be controlled and forced to do his dirty work. If only he had agreed to run away with me when I had asked him to. Before he found out about my betrayal. Was I being too innocent believing we could escape the violence? Have a normal life? Probably.

None of that mattered now, anyway. Romero would never forgive me. Once he was done with me, he would toss me out onto the street. I didn't want to return to my family. I was tired of being under the thumb of ruthless and immoral men. There had to be a better way.

"What are you doing?" Romero asked from the doorway.

"Oh!" I set my phone on the bed. "I didn't hear you come upstairs."

"Did you read the file?"

"I got in touch with Vincent."

"What did he say?"

"He didn't want me to talk about anything on the phone."

"Of course he didn't." Romero rolled his eyes. "His texts were so careful when you two were colluding behind my back. It's a good thing for me, you and Sandro weren't as careful. What do you think Vincent would to do his stupid, younger brother if he knew the two of you had been discussing your plan in texts?"

"Sandro tried to be careful." We shouldn't have discussed what I was doing to Romero so recklessly, but I needed someone to talk to. "It's my fault we got caught."

"You're at fault for so many things, aren't you?"

The only thing I was at fault for was not distancing myself from my criminal family long before they forced me into an arranged marriage with a killer.

"Take pictures of the file and pretend you went into my office and got it. Isn't that what you were doing before? Sneaking around like a little mouse and going through my private papers?"

Maybe if they were so private, you shouldn't have left them for me to find.

"Bring it to him as soon as you can." He motioned toward the file on the dresser.

"I'm going to meet with him this week."

"Perfect."

"What do these names and locations mean?"

"That's not really important." He came into the room and stood in front of me, towering over me, always reminding me how much stronger and in control of me he was. "The less you know, the more authentic it will seem. Besides, I can't trust that you won't slip and tell him something he doesn't need to know."

It wasn't like I wanted to help my family any more than I wanted to help Romero. I wanted them all to leave me alone and let me live in peace. All this stress and anxiety was taking a toll on me.

"I was looking at schools when you came in," I

offered, hoping to change the subject. "I could start in the fall."

Not that I wanted to be in this situation once the summer was over, but at least the prospect of an education gave me something to look forward to. I had to have a goal. Something to focus on while I navigated being in the middle of a deadly feud.

"The fall?"

"That's when the semester starts."

"I'm afraid that deal is off the table, sweetheart." He ran his fingers along the cherry wood of the dresser. "You're not going back to school."

"Why?" I lurched to my feet "You said I could finish my degree. You encouraged it and thought it was a good idea. You promised I could go to law school."

"That was before I knew you were fucking me over. Why would I support your dreams now? It isn't like you ever thought I was really your husband. Not the way I thought you would be my wife."

His words hurt more than they should have. He wasn't wrong. I walked down that aisle and said those vows, knowing I had no intention of really being his wife, but somehow that changed.

"Please, Romero. This is what I need. I have to have something to look forward to." I tried to hold back the tears, but his newest revelation crushed me. "I'll lose my mind."

"I guess you should have thought about that

before you came into my house and deceived me. You took my last name and pretended to want to build a life with me. You're far more dangerous than any enemy I've ever encountered. Now that I know that, I know how to handle you."

"When are you going to understand that I didn't have a choice?" I was tired of explaining this. "I didn't want to hurt you."

"You keep saying that," he shouted. "All you had to do was come to me and I would have protected you. Instead, you spied on me and brought crucial information to your family. Information that could get me killed in the hands of the wrong people, and it doesn't get more wrong than the Torrios."

"I didn't even know you when they forced me to marry you." I pointed at him. "What about you?"

"What about me?" He gestured in the air with his hand. "Please tell me what you think I did wrong in all of this?"

"You could have turned down their arrangement. If it didn't seem right to you, why didn't you refuse? Where were all your street smarts and business savvy then? Why did you give them an opening?"

"I had my reasons."

"What reasons?" I yelled. "Help me understand."

"I don't have to explain anything to you."

"I won't let you blame this all on me. It's bad enough you're holding me hostage. Now you won't let me finish my education? What did I do to deserve any of this?"

"That's a good question."

When he laughed, my nerves churned in the pit of my stomach. How much more of this was I expected to take?

"A question you'll have plenty of time to think about when you're waiting for me to give you the next bit of information to bring to your rotten family."

"I hate you." I didn't mean that, although I should have.

"Do you think I care about your feelings?" He gripped my arm and brought me to him. "Your actions have consequences. Do you know how lucky you are to still be breathing after the shit you pulled?"

"Just kill me then." I challenged him. "Death would be better than this."

Something shifted in his expression. Almost as if I had hurt him with my words. Why would he care if I thought I was better off dead?

"Do you want me to kill you?" He shook his head. "You stupid woman."

When he took my hips in his hands and tugged me closer to him, I tried to break out of his hold, but he was too strong.

"Don't provoke me." He ran his lips along my jaw

and to my ear. "You're alive because you serve a purpose. Don't forget that."

He held my face between his hands, lowering his head to press his mouth to mine. He shoved his tongue between my lips. I tensed when he squeezed my backside with his free hand. He roughly assaulted my lips, showing me who was in charge.

I pushed against his chest, but it was a weak attempt and he knew it. He kept kissing me, making me despise myself for giving into my desires. I twisted my fingers through his hair, breathing fast against his mouth.

When he lifted me up, I wrapped my legs around his waist. As he carried me to the bed, I kissed him with the same eagerness he'd shown me a few seconds ago.

He plopped me down on the bed and ran his fingers along my lips. I rose to my knees and reached for him, but he held up his hand, halting my response.

"You're forgetting which one of us is in control." He gazed around the room. "I'm having your things moved from my bedroom to this room."

His bedroom?

"It's our bedroom," I said.

"This is my house." He twirled a strand of my hair around his finger. "None of it belongs to you."

"You want me to sleep in here?"

"Did you honestly believe I'd share my bed with a traitor?"

"I'm not a traitor." I swatted his hand away from me. "I don't belong here."

"Yeah, and I'm not a criminal." He stepped away from me. "Get familiar with that file. Make sure you sell it to Vincent, because if he suspects that you're playing him the way you played me, you won't survive the week."

"You're a heartless son of a bitch," I shouted.

"Tell me something I don't know."

CHAPTER 4

Romero
Damn that woman! Why did she have such an influence over me? It would be so easy to fall back into bed with her. To start a new life that included only the two of us. The one where she asked me to run away with her. To leave this ugly world behind and relish in her beautiful soul. If there was ever anyone to yank me from this violent situation I willingly threw myself into, it was her.

Were we heading that way? I had opened up to her. Told her things about my family and my past that I had never shared with anyone. I wanted to give her the life she deserved. One where I was a good husband. The man who could protect her, provide for her, love her…

When I discovered her betrayal, I couldn't see straight. I couldn't think clearly. I thought it would be easier to hurt her. To make her feel worthless.

After telling her she couldn't go back to school, and seeing the anguish in her eyes, I realized I took no pleasure in hurting her. Her pain was my pain. *How the fuck did that happen?*

The absolute worse part of our most recent conversation was her admitting that she would rather be dead than stay with me. She wished for death. She wanted me to kill her.

Death would be better than this.

Those words would be etched in my mind for the rest of my life.

When I came into my study, Gio was standing by the window, scrolling through his phone. I shut the door and took a seat behind my desk.

"You look like shit," my brother said. "What the hell happened?"

"Fuck off."

"Seriously, what are you doing?"

"Running this empire."

"You're too distracted for that." He set his phone down on the charger on my desk. "You need to deal with your marriage and then you can worry about running this business. Right now, you're off, and if you don't take care of shit, you're going to get us killed."

"No one is getting killed."

"Really?"

"My marriage is a sham. She's being dealt with."

"By torturing her?" He sat across from me. "She's

been scared since the day she met you. I don't even know how to describe what she is now, but she's not strong enough for you."

"You don't know anything about her." Gio had a good sense of perception. He read people better than I could. He knew Luciana better than I'd liked. "She has to answer for her part in all of this."

"And then what?" Gio asked. "What happens to her once she has answered for her sins and served her purpose here?"

"I need to figure out which of the families we can trust. Once we settle the score with the Torrios, we'll need a plan in place if we still want to move our product through the New York channels."

"You didn't tell me your plans for Lu." He rested his chin on his hand. "Once the score is settled and all, what happens to her? Is she supposed to spend the rest of her days atoning for something that was never her fault to begin with?"

"What the fuck do you want from me?" I shouted. "Am I not entitled to take some time to digest what she did to me?" *Death would be better than this.* Her words echoed in my mind like a fucking punishment. "I don't know what I'm going to do with her."

Gio continued to press me with his icy blue stare.

"I should divorce her and throw her out on the street."

"You know what the consequences of that would be. You'd have to send her back to a family that never wanted her in the first place. If they had, she wouldn't be here."

"Once her family finds out that I know she was a plant, they'll disown her, possibly eliminate her."

"Can your conscience handle that?"

I didn't want her dead. I didn't enjoy hurting her even after she wounded me like no one else ever had. "I need time to process all of this, but in the meantime, there's no reason we can't use Luciana to bring false information to her scumbag family."

"It's a dangerous game for her to be playing." His disapproval of my plan was clear in his tone, his expression, and his words. "She's going to break under the stress. She's too fragile for this."

"The Torrios started it when they sent her here. They knew the risk they were taking when they put her in my path. The only difference now is, she has my protection, even if she doesn't know it."

"You care for her."

"What's on the agenda today?" I ignored his observation because admitting my feelings for my tainted wife would expose my weakness. What kind of message would I send if I didn't make her pay for her sins?

"Apparently not your love life." He laughed. "You should forgive her."

"You should mind your business."

"Fine."

"Let me worry about Luciana and you do your job." I clasped my fingers and rested my elbows on my desk. "What do you have for me?"

"You're now the proud owner of three new clubs. Two of them are being shut down and completely renovated to suit your new brand."

"As a thriving club owner in New York City?"

"Exactly."

"And the third?"

"Cantinos." He nodded. "You saw the profit from last month. That was is doing well."

"Can we trust the staff?"

"Mostly, but it can't hurt to vet a few of them. I'm running background checks now and I'm putting our guys in place to make sure everything is on the up and up."

"No one is on the take or stealing from me?"

"We'll know more in a day or two."

"Nicely done."

"Thanks."

"These clubs are what we need to stay off the FBI's radar. I need to establish us as more legitimate than ever before if we expect to keep growing the other businesses. I can't let anyone fuck this up for us."

"The Torrios?"

"I don't know why they're gunning for us, but we have to get ahead of them."

"We're already ahead of them. We figured out what they were up to."

"Yes, but not before I made an alliance with them. They know things about our business that they shouldn't."

"Maybe we should set up a meeting with Giancarlo."

"I want no more outsiders in."

"He was Dad's second. Since when have you consider him an outsider?"

"When he convinced me to marry into that family." I slammed my hand on my desk. "They took over Dad's territory two weeks after he died."

"You never cared about that before." He straightened his posture. "We never wanted Dad's territory."

"We were young. We didn't know who to trust. Giancarlo was all we had."

"He's an ally."

"I'm not saying that has changed, but the Torrios didn't really need an alliance with us. We needed them more than they needed us. I should have seen that."

"The cartel needed us to find a safe way to move their products."

"We could have found a way to get through the ports without Antonio." I ran my hand through my hair. "We moved too fast."

"What's done is done."

"A mistake we can't make again."

"We won't, but for now, no outside influence," Gio said. "It's me and you."

"I'm all in."

"I know."

"This has been bothering me." I tossed the file of Luciana's parents at him. "I want to pursue it."

"Why?"

"Someone murdered them, and Antonio didn't seek to avenge his sister's death." I picked up the file again. "That's not sitting well with me. It could be nothing, but I want to make sure."

"For you or for Lu?"

"You're not going to leave me alone about her, are you?"

"I need to know where you stand, where your head is. Wouldn't you do the same for me?"

"I hate to admit this, but you might be smarter than me."

"I know I'm smarter than you." He grinned. "I'm glad you finally see it."

"I don't think you would have jumped into this alliance as quickly as I had."

"I don't know." Gio shrugged. "If someone had dangled a woman as gorgeous as Luciana in front of me, I might have forgotten all of my business sense too."

My brother was no fool. I allowed my desires for Luciana to cloud my judgment. When she asked me why I hadn't walked away from the deal her uncle offered me, I could have told her the truth, but I didn't. I didn't know if I ever would.

"Just dig deeper."

"Do you think Antonio had Lu's parents killed?"

"I want to know why he would cover it up." I needed as much leverage as I could find if I was going to present a case to the other families to stand with me. Luciana's parents could be exactly what I needed.

"I'll see what I can find out. Give me a few days."

"Thank you." I glanced at my watch. "Tell the entourage we're going out tonight. I want full security detail. Tip off some of those rag social media sites who can't get enough of organized crime and tell them we'll be in the city."

"Where are we headed?"

"Cantinos." I smirked. "Call ahead and tell them they'll be entertaining my wife and I tonight, and several of my guests."

"You want the world to know you're a legitimate business owner."

"It's time we made a public appearance."

CHAPTER 5

Luciana

The crowded club intimidated me. There were hordes of people already inside, and a line three blocks long to get into this popular club. Romero and his group were ushered into the impressive building ahead of all the people waiting to get in, but no one made a comment or seemed annoyed. They must have known who Romero and Gio were.

The music blared out of the doorway but seemed to quiet as we entered a chic foyer area, covered in large mirrors and hardwood floors. Elaborate crystal chandeliers hung over our heads as we walked through the lobby. The place was stunning.

Another line formed to enter the club area, but we bypassed that one too. Everyone stared at us, but not because we were jumping ahead. It was obvious by the way they held up their phones and recorded us as we walked by, they knew who we were. Romero smiled at them, and Gio even kissed a few women as we made our way into the club.

The entire setting overwhelmed me. I'd gone out with Sandro once or twice when I turned twenty-one to places like this. My cousin had also achieved VIP status at most of the clubs and restaurants in the city. I didn't like the masses. I would much rather be home reading a book and soaking in a hot bath.

Not tonight, though. Tonight, I had to be on the arm of one of the most powerful men in the city. I had to keep quiet and pretend we were in a real relationship. From the snobby glances and the dirty looks I was getting from several Kardashian wannabes, I'd say I was doing a convincing job.

"Stay close to me." Romero wrapped his arm around my waist and guided me into the main area. "Unsavory people frequent these places."

"Then why did you buy it?"

"It'll make me a lot of money."

"Don't you already have a lot of money?"

"Compared to some, I suppose."

"Mr. Bilotti." A tall, attractive woman with long black hair and olive-colored skin approached us. Her face was flawlessly covered in makeup and her eyebrows were on point. Her long eyelashes fluttered when he smiled at her. "I'm Aria Martinez, the manager of Cantinos. It's a pleasure to finally meet you."

"The pleasure is all mine." Romero extended his hand without letting go of me with his other arm. "I've heard fantastic things about you and your ability to make this club such a success."

"I'm not afraid of hard work." She batted her eyelashes at him again and didn't readily let go of his hand. "I'm really looking forward to working with you and seeing where we can take this in the next few months."

What did she mean by 'this'?

"I'm here to check things out tonight, but I'd like to meet up later to discuss business." He gazed at me as he released her hand from his. "Aria, this is my beautiful wife, Luciana."

"Nice to meet you." She barely looked at me as she set her sights on Romero. *Is she drooling?* "I have so many ideas I can't wait to share with you. The last owner didn't have my vision, but I can already tell you and I have chemistry."

Are you kidding me?

"Expect to meet with me in the next few days to discuss our business plan." Romero pulled me closer to him.

Is he trying to show her he isn't interested in her?

I rested my head on his shoulder, inching closer to him, staking some twisted claim on a man who tried to kill me the other night. Why were we playing this game?

"Whatever you want." Aria smiled at him. "If you

need *anything*, let me know, and I do mean anything." She glanced at me and then back to him. "I'm at your disposal. You never know what we can come up with. Together."

As we walked away, Romero motioned Gio closer. "Monitor her. I'm not sure she's staying."

"This place is packed." Gio looked around. "I think she has something to do with that."

"There's something about her I don't like."

"She seemed to like you enough," I said.

"Maybe that's why I don't trust her. If she's bold enough to flirt with me in front of my wife, how can she have enough integrity to run my business?"

He ushered me over to a private area behind the bar. It was set up with tables and had a perfect view of the dance floor. The rest of the guys followed us, taking seats at the various high top tables. They surveyed the area, looking for threats and ways to make a quick exit if needed.

Romero slid out my chair and guided me into it. His tall, muscular form towered over me now that I was seated. I was like every other woman in this club. I couldn't take my eyes off him. He'd chosen to wear a dark gray suit that was custom to his spectacular body. The stubble that dusted his jaw and chin was as neatly maintained as the hair on his head. His sharp appearance accentuated his beautifully sculpted face and stunning green eyes. Women couldn't resist staring at him and snapping not-so-subtle selfies with him in the background. His dangerous reputation demanded respect. We'd only been here fifteen minutes, but I could see both the admiration and fear in the expression of the men we'd encountered. I could also see the lust and desire in the women who caught a glimpse of him. Some of them didn't even care that they were here on a date. I had a feeling they would drop their dates in a heartbeat if Romero asked them to. They would drop their panties too.

"Are you jealous?"

"Of the successful Latino goddess with the long legs, big boobs, and luscious hair? Why would I be?"

"She has nothing on you." He cupped my face in his hand. "I prefer your beauty and unaltered boobs over all that plastic surgery any day. If you wore that much makeup, I'd scrub it off until I found the real you."

"Oh." I swallowed hard under his intense gaze. Did he really mean that, or was he being cruel by making me think he was still interested in me?

"You do know she was not so delicately telling me that if I wanted to include you in any activities, she'd be open to having you join us."

"What?" I fidgeted with the hem of my dress.

"Learn to read the signs, sweetheart." He released my face and took a seat across from me. "Gio, order us a round of drinks," he yelled across the small area. "I'll have the best vodka we have and

Luciana will have a glass of the most expensive champagne. Let's see if the prices they charge are worth it."

"You don't think I would ever want to do anything like that, do you?" The heat rose up my neck and spread to my cheeks. "I couldn't."

"I wouldn't share you." He winked. "Not even with a woman."

I nodded, feeling relieved he didn't want to entertain Aria's offer. But I was also confused. After everything that had happened between us, did he still consider me his wife?

We sat at the table for an hour. I sipped my second glass of champagne as people came over and introduced themselves to Romero. Most were employees at the club. Others wanted a chance to see him. My husband was very charismatic. If I didn't know better, I would have thought he was running for office. He was sophisticated and charming, and everyone seemed so intrigued by him, including me.

He smiled at the men and told them how beautiful their wives or girlfriends were. He occasionally reached across the table and took my hand when he introduced me to people I wouldn't remember the next day.

From an outsider's point of view, we appeared to be the perfect couple. If they only know what occurred behind closed doors.

Gio joined us at the table. "How are you holding up, beauty?"

"It's a little loud in here, but the place has a good vibe." I finished my drink as I glanced at Romero holding a conversation with a server. "He seems pleased."

"Do you want another drink?" Gio asked.

"I'm okay for now." I looked around the bar. "I'm going to find the bathroom."

When I stood, Romero got up and came to stand next to me. "Where are you going?"

"The ladies' room," I said.

"Gio and I need to take a quick meeting in the back." He motioned toward the bar. "I won't be long."

"I'll be fine."

"Jag." He called for my guard to join us. "Luciana needs to use the restroom. Make sure she gets there safely, and no one fucks with her."

"I can find the bathroom myself," I mumbled, knowing I'd be overruled.

"It's his job," Romero said into my ear. "Don't fight me on this."

"Come on, Lu." Jag guided me across the crowded bar area. "I think there were some restrooms off the lobby. The ones in the club will be too crowded."

"You're probably right," I yelled over the music.

Her Heartless King

As we made our way out of the loud club and to the lobby, I breathed a sigh of relief.

"This isn't your kind of place, is it?" Jag asked. "I've been watching you. Well, it's my job to watch you. I'm not being creepy."

"I know." I laughed. "You're right. I don't do the club scene. I like being home."

"With your books and your movies."

"You're getting to know me well."

"I know there was some trouble the other day with you and the boss," he said.

"You do?" Did they all know I had betrayed Romero for my family?

"Some of the guys know when there's trouble in the house and we know Mr. Bilotti didn't come home for a few days."

"He didn't." I wondered where Romero had been for those forty-eight hours. Was he alone? Did I have any right to be upset if he had found company with a woman who didn't betray him?

"I'm not trying to pry."

"I don't think you're prying. I appreciate your concern."

"I wanted to say that he's not a bad person. He's harsh and can be really frightening."

"Tell me about it."

"But he's fair." He walked me toward the bathroom. "I shouldn't be saying anything at all, but I wanted you to know when he gets too intense or you need a break, I'm around even if you want to go for a ride and get away for a while. I work for Mr. Bilotti, but I'm here for you, too. I get that being around his business could be stressful."

"That's sweet of you." I patted his arm. "Maybe I'll take you up on it, but right now I have to use the ladies' room."

"I'll wait right here."

"It's okay." I headed down the empty hall to the bathrooms. "I'll meet you at the club entrance. Go enjoy the music."

"I'll be right at the entrance."

The whole evening had been so overwhelming. I appreciated his words, but I needed a few minutes to be alone. Jag made the right call. Now that the live band had started everyone was inside the club and these bathrooms were line free. I welcomed the quiet atmosphere. If I could stay in here for the rest of the evening, I would, but I was certain Romero would barge in and pull me out in ten minutes.

After I freshened up and reapplied my lipstick, I decided I had spent a reasonable amount of time decompressing. As I walked down the hall back toward the club entrance, a tall man came toward me. I thought little of it as I looked down at the floor and continued on my way, but as I tried to pass him, he stopped in front of me, blocking my way.

"Excuse me," I tried to get around him, looking

over his shoulder and seeking out Jag. Why did I tell him he could leave me?

"Lu," the man said.

When I finally made eye contact with him, I recognized him immediately. His chestnut eyes and dark hair were the same as I remembered, but his face had matured into a man. Not the teenager I remembered. "Carson?"

"I wasn't sure you would remember me." When he smiled, I remembered the crush I used to have on him. "It's been a few years."

"Yeah." I tucked my hair behind my ear. "I'm surprised you remember me. We didn't interact much at school. Weren't you two years ahead of me?" I knew he was. He ran track and most of the girls had a thing for him.

"I believe so." He nodded. "How have you been?"

"Good."

Well, not really that good. I graduated from school and had to come back home to my mafia family and my nasty aunt who hates me. They let me go to school to become a paralegal so I could file their paperwork and bring them coffee. When I finally got up the nerve to ask if I could go to law school, they forced me into an arranged marriage with an arms dealer who tried to kill me, and now I'm his prisoner.

"Real good. How about you?"

"I'm doing well. I'm an agent in the New York bureau."

"An agent?"

"FBI."

"Oh." *Wonderful.* "That's impressive."

"When I graduated from college, a year earlier than expected, I enrolled in the academy and worked hard, and here I am."

"What brings you to the club?" As if I didn't know.

"I heard a big player in the organized crime outfit bought this place and that raises all kinds of red flags. This guy is definitely someone this city doesn't need."

"Really?" *You should probably get used to him because he's not going anywhere.*

"I came to check things out. His name is Romero Bilotti. I can only speculate what he's going to try to move through this club. Weapons, drugs, sex trafficking... he's bad news for this city. Have you heard of him?"

"He's my husband."

"You're kidding. I know you're a Torrio but—"

"Actually, Agent Morgan." Romero seemed to appear out of nowhere and he looked like a raging bull ready to charge. "She's a Bilotti."

CHAPTER 6

Romero

My body filled with fury, but I couldn't react. Not the way I wanted to. Carson Morgan had one job... to bring men like me down. It didn't take him long to get here.

"Romero." Luciana came to stand next to me without me having to tell her to. *Encouraging.* "I went to school with Carson."

"Really?" I stared him down. "What a small world."

"Hello, Mr. Bilotti." Carson's gaze followed my hand as I took Luciana's in mine.

Don't look at my wife.

"I heard you own this establishment, so I thought I'd come by and check it out."

"I'm flattered." I tightened my grip on Luciana's hand, trying to keep my composure. She must have sensed my aggression, because she inched closer to me. "I'll let the bar know you're my guest."

"That's generous, but I'm on duty."

"Of course you are." The ink was barely dry on the sale for this place and already the Feds were up my ass. "Perhaps another night, then. Bring guests. I'm sure you'll find Cantinos to be everything you're not expecting."

"I'm sure it's more than I could have imagined."

"I hope we don't disappoint you." I let go of Luciana's hand and wrapped my arm around her waist. "If you'll excuse us, my wife and I have other people to greet."

"I'm sure you'll be seeing more of me." Carson's eyes narrowed.

"I look forward to it." I ushered Luciana down the hall and toward a back staircase before she could say goodbye.

As we hurried up the steps, she said nothing. My guess was she was trying to keep pace with me. With each step forward, my rage intensified. It was one thing to have the Feds come to investigate what I was up to, especially since I'd purchased a popular club. That was expected. It was an entirely different scenario that he had approached my wife.

I opened the large, double oak doors that had shuddered my new office. After guiding Luciana inside, I pulled the heavy doors closed.

"A fucking FBI agent?" I shouted. "Of all the

people you could have gone to school with, now you've caught the attention of a Fed?"

"I, I didn't do anything wrong." Panic rose in her voice when I stepped toward her. "I only went to the ladies' room. Carson approached me. I didn't know who he was at first."

"What did he want?"

"He asked if I knew you, and I told him you were my husband."

"That's it?" I studied her for a moment. "Why are you so afraid, then? Is this another fucking set up?"

"What?" She backed away from me. "No."

"You're not convincing me."

"It's just that I don't..." She instinctively placed her hand on her throat, reminding me of the animal that I was. "I don't want you to hurt me." She wiped the tear that slipped from her eye away. "Please," she whispered. "I didn't do anything."

For fuck's sake. I gave her PTSD. Gio was right. She wasn't strong enough for me. But that was the same with her family. I was all she had. I needed her to be able to handle me, even at my worst.

When I reached for her hand, she stumbled back, but I caught her and brought her closer to me.

"Relax." I held her against me, noting how fast her heart beat. "I don't like when you're this jittery."

"I haven't seen him since high school. I had no idea he was an FBI agent until he told me tonight. I was only with him for a few minutes."

"That can never happen again."

"It won't."

"You're sure he didn't ask you anything?"

"Even if he had, I wouldn't have told him anything."

"Good girl." I stroked her hair before stepping back. "That attitude deserves a reward."

Her eyes darted to my hand as I reached around and took my gun out of the back of my pants and set it on the desk behind me. I slipped my suit jacket off and tossed it on the chair in the corner of the room.

"Have I told you how spectacular you look tonight?" I loosened my tie, admiring the way she looked in the short, black sleeveless dress she had worn. "I had to refrain myself from shooting several men this evening for looking at you the wrong way."

She licked her lips when I unbuckled my belt.

"Take your dress off."

"Here?" She glanced over her shoulder at the door. "What if someone comes in?"

"No one would dare." I unbuttoned my pants. "Take your dress off."

She bit her lip, debating, but I wasn't asking.

"I won't *tell* you again." I moved toward her. "I'll just rip it off you."

She hesitantly slipped the thin straps over other shoulders before reaching to her side and unzipping the dress. I palmed my cock when she shimmied the silky black material over her waist and down her legs.

"Leave your heels on."

She stepped out of the dress, standing before me in a tiny black thong and a pair of high silver stilettos.

"You're perfect."

She rocked back and forth as she fidgeted with her hands.

"You need to settle down." I moved close to her. "You're supposed to be enjoying this."

"Can you kiss me?"

"Is that what you want?" I trailed my mouth along her jaw and to her lips. "Here?"

She nodded.

Tracing my finger down her throat and to her breasts, I circled her nipple, making it peak before working my way down her stomach.

"How about here?" I dropped to my knees and pressed my face against her mound, breathing in her scent. Sliding my hand up the back of her leg, I placed it on her ass, gripping it as I slid her panties to one side with my free hand. "Can I kiss here?"

She bucked her hips forward and let out a soft moan when I glided the tip of my tongue along her clit. Slowly swirling along her wet folds, I kissed her long and deep. She raked her fingers through my hair when I squeezed her backside.

I could lick her for hours, but my cock had other

ideas. When I abruptly stood, she didn't flinch. She draped her arms around my neck and kissed my mouth, shoving her tongue inside mine and tasting where I had been. *That's fucking hot.*

"What should I do with you next?" I reached between us and lowered my zipper. "Do you want me to fuck you?"

"Yes."

"Do you think you deserve my cock?"

"I do." She slinked her hand between our heated bodies, taking my dick in her firm grasp and pumping fast. "But I'll do whatever you want."

"Because you're mine." I lifted her in my arms and slammed her against the door, holding her captive as she wrapped her legs around my hips. "Only mine."

I tried to shake the vision of her standing in that dark hallway, talking to that sleazy agent. The way he eyed her up infuriated me. No one would ever have her like this.

I twisted her thong between my fingers and tore it from her with one swift action. Her eyes enlarged and a harsh gasp escaped her lungs, but she didn't protest as I rammed inside her waiting sex. Her back hit the door with a loud thud when I thrusted as deeply as I could.

"You're so tight for me." The faster I flexed my hips, the harder I pounded into her. "I'm the only one who will ever take any pleasure from your body."

When she held onto me for support, the anger and frustration of the past few days seemed to dissipate, leaving just the two of us. I wanted more than anything to go back and handle the situation differently, but it was too late for regrets. I had to stay the course and make things right. No matter the cost.

"Romero." She tightened her hold on my waist with her quivering thighs.

"Come for me," I breathed against her lips. "Just as I'm the only one who will take from you, I'm also the only one who will ever give you this pleasure."

"I know." She slithered her hands under my shirt and clawed at my back. "I don't want anyone else."

Even after hearing the words uttered from her lips, I didn't believe her. She had so much to atone for. Would I let her?

I thrust into her, holding still as she clenched around my cock. She shuddered into me as she stroked my cheek. When she opened her eyes and stared into mine, I let go of all the betrayal and deception and allowed myself to be her husband, even if only for this brief encounter. Groaning and holding her tight, I released inside her until I was empty and sated.

I lowered her feet to the floor, but she clung to me.

"You should get dressed." I pressed my forehead

to hers. "Gio is going to meet me here in a few minutes."

When I released her from my hold, she steadied herself against the door. If I didn't have business to tend to, I would have taken her again.

I scooped her dress off the floor and handed it to her. "Get dressed."

She took it, turning her back to me as she stepped into it. I tucked my shirt into my pants and straightened it out before fixing my tie. I scooped her torn thong from the floor and shoved it in my pocket.

"What goes in has to come out." I took a couple of tissues from the box on the desk. "You might need these."

"Thanks." The blushed filled her cheeks when she faced me, taking the tissues I had offered.

"Jag will take you home."

"Aren't you coming with me?"

"I have some business to take care of." I put my jacket on. "I'll be home later."

"Business with her?" She raised her voice.

"What does that mean?" I picked up my gun from the desk and tucked it in the back of my pants. "What do you think I'm going to do with her?"

"Whatever you want."

"Are you seriously picking a fight with me now?" I grabbed her arm and tugged her to me. "What's wrong with you?"

"I, nothing." Her shoulders sagged. "I'll go home with Jag."

"Do you believe I would do what we just did and then... and then what?" I squeezed her arm. "Fuck the club manager?"

Why did her opinion of me matter?

"When I said our vows, they meant something to me." I let go of her arm and opened the door. "Jag," I yelled down the hall for her guard.

"Romero," she whispered, but I ignored her.

"Take Luciana home," I said to Jag when he appeared in the doorway.

"Sure thing, boss," he said.

"Do not let her out of your sight until she's in the house." I widened the door. "If you do, I'll break your neck. Are we clear?"

"I'll get her home safe and sound." He backed away from me. "I swear."

Luciana moved past me, not even bothering to say goodbye. Wasn't I the one who should be mad at her? *Hell!* Figuring out my wife was one of the most difficult tasks I'd ever encountered. Maybe I should forget about this plan and cut her loose.

"Hey." Aria stood in the doorway with a bottle of vodka and two glasses. Well, fuck, my wife was barely out of the room and this one was ready to entertain. "I wanted to give you a proper welcome."

She shimmied by me and placed the bottle and glasses on the desk. She turned around and sat on the edge, crossing her legs and pushing her chest out. The scent of the room was fresh with the sex I'd just had with Luciana and this one was trying to seduce me.

"I saw your wife leaving," she said. "She couldn't hang?"

"There's no reason for her to be here all night while I make sure my club is stable and making me money."

"I can assure you it is very stable and extremely lucrative." She uncrossed her legs, leaving them slightly spread, so I could see her red panties. "I thought we could go over all the benefits and perks you'll experience as the new owner."

"What benefits would those be?" I stepped closer to her. "I'm curious."

"I thought you might be." She bit her over-filled bottom lip, but it wasn't nearly as sexy as when Luciana did it. "I brought you your favorite vodka."

"Is that a perk?"

"The perk is having a drink with me." She licked her lips. "How thirsty are you?"

"Oh." I stepped closer to her. "I'm extremely thirsty."

"I thought so."

"I'm thirsty for power, money, and control." I extended my hand to her and helped her off the desk. "I crave loyalty, honor, and trust. I expect it from the people who work for me."

"You'll get all of that from me and more."

"Do you know what I'm not thirsty for?"

"What?"

"A woman who respects me so little that she thinks I would betray my wife five minutes after she leaves the building."

"I don't think that."

"Really?" I grabbed her arm and pulled her toward me. "Let me tell you what else I don't like."

She tried to struggle out of my hold, but I tightened my grip. She was about to see the real me.

"I don't care for anyone who disrespects my wife. You've done that twice tonight."

"No, I thought that…"

"That I'd want to fuck you because you spread your legs for me and let me see your cheap panties?"

"I'm sorry."

"I don't think you are, but you will be."

"This was a misunderstanding." She looked into my eyes and hers were wide with worry. "I've entertained a lot of guys like you through the years. Strong and powerful gangsters. They all have no problem cheating on their wives or girlfriends. Most of them have side-pieces. I thought you would be the same."

"You thought wrong." I flung her arm away. "Those men you speak of have no honor. No integrity. If you knew my wife, you would know there's no reason for me to cheat on her, especially not with someone like you."

She rolled her eyes.

"Am I wrong?"

"You don't know anything about me."

"You've known me all of ten minutes. I'm your new boss. Didn't anyone ever tell you about first impressions?" I held up my hand. "You know what, I'm going to forget this happened because you seem to make my club a lot of money, but if you ever make my wife feel uncomfortable or come at me again, I promise you, sweetheart, the only job you're going to find yourself in is seating people at a diner in Hoboken."

She didn't say anything.

"Are we clear?"

"Yes."

"Now get out of my office and go do your job." I pointed to the doorway, where Gio was now standing. "You can leave the vodka."

She huffed as she put her head down and stormed out of the room.

"Well, that didn't take long." Gio entered the room and shut the door. "You pissed off your manager."

"She might not be that for long, and she pissed me off first." I poured two glasses of vodka. "I don't trust her."

"Well, you can't blame her for trying." Gio took a glass from me. "That didn't shock me at all."

"Something else shocked you?" I sipped the vodka, noting Aria had good taste in liquor.

"You could say that."

"Don't keep me in suspense."

"I caught the tail end of your encounter with Aria and I was surprised how hard you defended Luciana." He shrugged. "I didn't think you cared that much."

"I'm not discussing this with you." My defense of Luciana caught me off guard, too. "We have a bigger problem."

"What?"

"The Feds."

"Yeah, I saw a few of them in the club tonight."

"I found one with Luciana."

"What? Who?"

"Carson Morgan." I finished my drink and poured another. "They went to high school together."

"Hmm." Gio took out his phone and started scrolling. "That didn't come up in any of her background information."

"She says she hasn't seen him since then. He's a few years older than her."

"Do you think their meeting was a coincidence?"

"I sure as fuck hope so, because if she's working with the Feds…"

"She wouldn't do that," Gio said.

"We didn't think she'd be working with her family either."

"True."

"We have to be absolutely sure." I handed him the bottle of vodka. "I trusted her a little too quickly last time and look how that turned out."

"I don't think Lu is the problem, but I have a feeling Agent Morgan is going to be a thorn in our side."

"Not if we take care of him quickly."

CHAPTER 7

Luciana

I came downstairs to movement in the kitchen. Could Romero be making me breakfast? The last time he made me his mother's French toast, he opened up a little. If he was making me breakfast, maybe he was willing to forgive me.

Wishful thinking.

He could hold a grudge. It must be all that Sicilian blood streaming through his veins.

We needed to make a connection. Other than the obvious sexual chemistry the two of us shared, there had to be more to this relationship. If we could move past what I had done and my family would let me live my life with the man they forced me to marry, maybe I would have a shot.

As I made my way to the kitchen, a flutter of hope bloomed inside me. If we had a meal together, we could talk, and I could try to explain to him I never meant to hurt him. Since he was cooking me breakfast, perhaps he was extending an olive branch. Maybe we could make this work after all.

"Good morning." I burst into the room, surprised to find an unfamiliar woman standing by the stove.

What the hell?

"Hello." She turned to face me. "You must be Luciana."

"Ah, yeah." I looked around at all the pots and pans on the counters of the normally immaculate kitchen. "And you are?"

"I'm Stella." She came to greet me with an extended hand. "Romero hired me to cook and help around the house."

"Oh." I shook her hand, admiring her silky black hair and flawless skin. She appeared to be about twenty years older than me, if I had to guess. Her slender figure and toned arms made me think she worked out a lot. She wore black yoga pants, a lavender t-shirt, and the coolest purple Converse sneakers.

"You seemed surprised to find me here," she said. "Didn't your husband tell you I was starting today?"

"It must have slipped his mind." Between trying to kill me and making me betray my family, he had been distracted. "It's nice to meet you."

"Same, Luciana." She tied an apron around her waist. "I'm familiarizing myself with the kitchen and all these fancy appliances. The possibilities are endless here."

"It is a beautiful kitchen." *We don't use it much, but we had sex on the center island once.* "You can call me Lu."

"Your husband always refers to you by your full name. I didn't realize you shortened it."

"Romero is the only one who refers to me as Luciana." Come to think of it, I didn't think he ever called me Lu. "You can do whatever you're comfortable with."

"If you like Lu, that's what I'll call you."

Hmm, why would such a pleasant woman want to work for Romero? Because he charmed her with his sexy smile and his mesmerizing eyes. Not to mention, he was probably paying her a small fortune to be here.

"Did you answer an ad?"

"To work here?" She laughed. "Romero doesn't seem like the kind of guy who puts an ad on the internet looking for help."

No." When I giggled, the sound seemed so foreign. "I guess he isn't."

"He's friends with my father."

"Oh."

"My dad used to work for Romero's dad as a landscaper many years ago back when I was in high school. I remember going to their house and being so impressed by the size." She shook her head.

"Romero was young back then. I babysat for him and Gio a few times after their mother passed away."

"Do you remember their mother?"

"No." She thought for a moment. "I think she passed away before I met them."

"Anyway, I went away to college and hadn't really seen Romero around. He left the area for a while. He's been really good to my dad through the years. When my dad mentioned I was looking for work, Romero suggested I come here and help."

"Are you a chef?"

"One upon a time." She pushed a few buttons on the oven. "I worked in a few restaurants in the city. I took some time off to raise my kids, but now all three of them are in college. Two are at Princeton and one at NYU."

"You must be so proud."

"I am." She beamed. "But now, I need to find myself again."

"I get it."

"You're being polite." She studied me. "You're young and newly married. You have your whole life ahead of you."

"I guess." *If my husband or my family doesn't kill me first.*

"We can plan the dinner menu when you have time," she said.

"I have nothing but time." *Since I don't have a job and I can't go to school.*

Why am I so pathetic?

"Good, because Romero has asked me to teach you to cook."

"He did?"

"He said you wanted to learn." She pulled her long, glossy hair into a ponytail with a purple band that matched her sneakers. "I thought that was so sweet of him."

"I can't cook much."

"We'll fix that."

The doorbell chimed throughout the house.

"I can get that," Stella said.

"No, that's okay." I backed toward the hallway. "You look busy here. I'll get it."

"When you get back, we can start on the menu."

"Okay." For the first time in days, I had something to look forward to. A fresh face in the house and it wasn't a big, burly, intimidating bodyguard.

When I opened the front door, my fleeting positive feeling dropped right to the bottom of my gut.

"Carson" *This isn't good.*

"Hello, Lu." He smiled. "You look surprised to see me."

"I am." I slipped out of the door and stood on the porch. I had a feeling Romero would not want him in the house. "I thought you worked in the city."

"I'm a federal agent." He shrugged. "I go where my cases lead me."

"What leads you here?"

"You."

"I don't understand." My throat constricted making it hard to swallow. "What could you possibly need with me?"

"It surprised me to see you last night." He leaned against the railing. "Even more surprised that you were married to Romero."

"Why?"

"You don't strike me as his type."

"I don't?" When I bit my thumbnail, I drew his gaze to my mouth. "You don't even know me, so how could you know what kind of man would be my type?"

"I remember you from school. You were shy. You kept to yourself, and didn't want to talk about your family. I can understand why."

"Do you have a point to any of this?"

"I did some investigating." He moved closer to me, so I inched back until I hit the door.

"I'm not sure I like where this is heading," I said. "It feels inappropriate."

"I know who your family is, and your marriage didn't sit well with me."

"My marriage is none of your business." Sometimes, I wished it was none of my business. "You shouldn't be here."

"Because it will make Romero mad?"

"Because you don't have any reason to be here."

"I'm not afraid of him." He pushed his sunglasses on top of his head.

You should be.

"But I think you are," he said.

"You would be wrong." *I'm a liar, but I didn't need an FBI agent in the middle of my already complicated life.*

"The makeup didn't cover the bruises on your neck." He nodded toward my throat. "Want to explain how they got there?"

"Maybe I like it rough." I touched my throat. "Again, it's none of your business."

"Take this." He reached into his inside suit pocket and took out a business card. "I want you to know I can get you out of whatever this is."

No, you can't.

"There are places you can go where you'll be protected." He pushed the card into my hand. "That's a private line to me. They'll put you through as soon as you call."

"I don't need to be protected."

"You're fooling yourself."

"You have to go now."

"You come from a dangerous family. If I had to guess, I'd say they forced you into this marriage because the girl I knew from school wouldn't marry Romero Bilotti willingly."

"I'm not that girl from school anymore." I glanced down at his business card. "You don't know anything about me, and if I were you, I wouldn't taunt my husband by using me."

Enough people are already using me.

"I'm here to investigate."

"What are you investigating?"

"The disappearance of four men who were associated with your husband."

I remembered the four men in the woods. I recalled in great detail what happened to two of them. Had the other two met the same fate?

"I don't know anything about my husband's business dealings."

"Would you like me to fill you in?"

Before I could answer, Romero and Gio pulled into the driveway. I quickly shoved Carson's card into my pocket. Romero glared at me from the passenger seat window. That feeling in the pit of my stomach when I answered the door to find Carson standing on the porch was nothing compared to the unsettled commotion going on in my gut now.

"Perfect timing," he said.

For who?

CHAPTER 8

Romero

"What the fuck is he doing here?" I reached for the door handle, but Gio held me back.

"You need to calm down and not do anything stupid." Gio nodded to the unmarked car at the bottom of the driveway with another agent waiting inside. "Morgan's not dumb. He didn't come here alone."

"He's not dumb? Then why is he on my porch talking to my wife? And what the hell is wrong with my wife? I told her she couldn't have any contact with him."

I exited the car and hurried up the walkway, trying to shove back the anger that wanted to erupt into a nasty inferno. Once I reached them, Luciana distanced herself from Carson. She fidgeted with her hands when I walked up the steps. I'd deal with her later.

"Agent Morgan," I took a breath. "What brings you here?"

"I have a few questions," he said.

"Not without an attorney present." Gio joined us. "You should know better than that, Agent Morgan."

"Luciana." I opened the front door. "Go inside."

She nodded and then disappeared into the house without saying goodbye to Carson.

"I didn't know arranged marriages were still a thing," Carson said. "With it being the twenty-first century and all."

"Believe whatever you want, but she is my wife," I reminded him. "If I find you around her again, it won't end well."

"Is that a threat?"

"Not at all." I clenched my fist, holding back the urge to punch that smug smirk off his face. "It's merely a fact. Luciana has nothing to do with anything that you would be concerned with."

"What is it you think I'd be concerned with?"

"Why are you here?" Gio got between us in an attempt to get me to shut up. "If you did your job last night, you would know that the club checked out. We're not breaking any laws."

"I wanted to check on Luciana."

"Why? I asked.

"I noticed the bruising on her neck lat night," he said. "It didn't sit well with me."

Fuck! This arrogant piece of shit came to my house to see my wife?

"Luciana doesn't concern you. If you have a legal reason to be here, take it up with my attorney." I nodded toward the car he came in. "Otherwise, you're trespassing, and I don't think your superiors would appreciate you harassing me."

"You're not above the law," Carson said.

"I never said I was." I had people on the take in his office, but I wasn't going to call in any favors yet. "If you approach my wife again, that badge won't mean much to me, Agent Morgan."

"I'd watch what you say to a federal agent." He pointed at me. "Someone might take it the wrong way."

"You wouldn't have to take it anyway if you'd get off my property," I raised my voice. "Contact my attorney if you have any further questions."

"Have a nice day, gentlemen," Carson said. "I'm sure our paths will cross again."

Gio stood directly in front of me so I couldn't chase that motherfucker down the steps and kill him.

"He better stay away from Luciana," I shouted.

"You better calm down." Gio waited for the agents to leave the property. "We cannot take out a fucking federal agent."

"Investigate him." I opened the door and barreled down the hallway. "Find the weakness."

The laughter coming from the kitchen stopped me just as I barged in. Luciana seemed so relaxed with Stella, but once she detected my presence, her smile fled. That smile I so desperately wanted to claim as my own.

I hired Stella because I thought she could offer Luciana comfort. Someone to connect with and confide in. My wife had no friends, no sisters, and no maternal figure. Her life was far too lonely and I was no help. She needed a motherly influence in her life.

"I need to speak with you," I said.

"We're planning dinner for the week," she told me.

"You can do that later." I took her by the arm and led her up the back staircase to the master bedroom.

She wiggled out of my hold when we approached the room.

"I don't think you should treat me that way in front of Stella." She adjusted her shirt that had slipped down her shoulder. "It's embarrassing."

"What did he want?" When I slammed the door, she jumped. "Why was he here?"

"I don't know." She backed away from me.

Minutes ago she was laughing and at ease, and now she looked as if she wanted to flee out a window. Her demeanor should have made me less intense. I sensed how afraid she was of me, but I couldn't rein it in.

"Stay still." I pinned her against the wall,

annoyed that my presence had such a terrifying reaction from her.

She wiped the hair from her face, looking anywhere but into my eyes.

"Why is he sniffing around you?"

"Because I'm married to you." She sighed. "He didn't give me a second glance in high school."

"Did you want him to?" Hell, did she have a thing for him?

"No."

"Do me a favor," I said. "From now on don't answer the door. We have people who do that."

"Fine." She rolled her eyes. "One more thing I can't do in my own house."

"Are you sure he didn't say anything?"

"Last night, he said you were a sex trafficker."

"Fuck him." I'd done plenty of illegal shit in my time, but I wouldn't get myself involved in sex trafficking.

"Is it true? Are you using the club to make women slaves?"

"You believe him?"

"I'm asking you."

"I'm a lot of things, Luciana, but I'm not that." When I thought back to the abuse my mother endured at my father's hands and how he degraded her and hurt her every chance he got, it infuriated me. "I wouldn't do that to any woman."

"I believe you." She relaxed her stance.

"Thank you." I softened my tone. "Did he say anything else?"

"He told me he is investigating the disappearance of four men." She wriggled her hands. "He didn't say who, but it's those men in the woods, isn't it?"

"He's fishing." I made it a point to tie up any loose ends with questionable business. There was no way they could tie any of that back to me. "He has nothing on me."

"I was in the woods. I witnessed what you... well, you know."

"Those men were working with your uncle to bring me down." In the last day, I found out those associates were responsible for Arturo's death. I took care of the remaining two, but I wouldn't make Luciana any more of an accomplice than she needed to be. "Agent Morgan doesn't want my presence in the city. Having someone like me running a successful business sends a message that the Feds no longer have control over the mob."

"Are you using the club for other purposes?"

"The club is one hundred percent legitimate."

"It seemed to be doing really well. Maybe that's something you could pursue."

"Instead of organized crime?" I laughed, but I admired her determination to find her way out of this life, but she needed to understand she couldn't take me with her. "That's never going to happen."

"You never know."

When she smiled, I took her chin between my fingers, and dropped my gaze to her mouth.

"I like when you smile."

"So you've told me before."

"You don't believe me?"

"I don't get many opportunities to do it when I'm around you." She bit her lip when I brought my mouth closer to hers. "Why does it have to be so complicated?"

"It didn't have to be this way." I brushed my lips along hers. "I don't want it to be this way."

"Can't we start over?"

"I wish."

I tightened my hold on her chin and kissed her waiting mouth, savoring the taste and indulging in her warmth. She relaxed into my hold, dropping her tense shoulders and wrapping her arms around my neck. She clung to me with such desire. Her need to be close to me, for me to hold her, and protect her could make me forget everything else. Only, I was far too stubborn for that.

I broke the kiss and stepped away. I turned my back to her so I wouldn't see the hurt in her expression. She weakened my defenses and made me far less ruthless when it came to her.

"Not today, butterfly." I cleared my throat. "I gave you a freebie last night."

"You said you didn't want it to be this way."

"What I want and what it is are two different things." I spun around to face her again. "Right now, I need you to set up that meeting with your family. I'm going to text you some pictures that they will think I left out on my desk."

"You want me to give it to them?"

"I also want you to tell them the death of Arturo has really screwed me up. See if any of them give you any sign of why they would take out one of my top soldiers."

"What if they won't give me anything?"

"Don't push them. If you ask too many questions, they will suspect what you're doing." I hated to put her in this position, but it was the only way for me to get inside the Torrio house and figure out what they were up to. "Although I never suspected you."

"I never pumped you for information."

"No, you just spied on me and went through my stuff when I wasn't home."

"Are we done?"

"For now."

"Can I go back downstairs?"

I nodded as she turned toward the door. She couldn't get out of the room fast enough. Did I hurt her feelings? Was she about to cry and she didn't want me to see?

I plopped down on the bed and stared at the ceiling. Why did I bring up her spying on me? When I was with her, I wanted to forget what she had done.

Her betrayal cut deep. If she were anyone else, she'd be dead. If an enemy had spied on me, I'd have shown no mercy.

But she wasn't an enemy. She was my wife. The woman I vowed to protect and spend the rest of my days with. Someone I envisioned a future with. The person I wanted to cherish. I wanted to make her laugh and give her anything her heart desired. I imagined what it would be like to fill her belly with babies. We could live the best life and have an incredible future. There was only one problem...

I don't know how to forgive you, Luciana.

CHAPTER 9

Luciana

Once Jag and I were through the gates of the Torrio estate, he walked me up the path and to the front door. When we got to the porch, my nerves kicked into overdrive. I had little desire to see my family, especially my aunt.

"There's a storm brewing," Jag looked up at the dark clouds. "The wind is kicking up."

"It looks pretty ominous." I doubt it would be any less threatening inside.

"I'll be over there." He pointed to the side driveway where the guards parked the cars. "Text me if you need me."

"I'll be fine." As long as I could deliver the false information with no one suspecting I was betraying them. If they figured out what I was doing, then I wouldn't be fine.

I rang the bell because I wasn't sure if I should

walk in. It didn't seem like my house anymore. Did it ever?

When Sandro answered, a sense of relief blanketed me. A face that was actually happy to see me.

"Lu?" He widened the door to let me in. "What are you doing here?"

"I, um, I'm here to see Vincent." My stomach flipped and my throat grew drier with each word I spoke. "He didn't tell you I was coming?"

"No." He hugged me. "It's nice to see you."

"It's good to see you, too."

"How are things going with the neanderthal?"

"Sandro." I shook my head. "Romero is not that bad. We're the ones who betrayed him, remember?"

"*Betrayed*?" He headed down the hall. "Aren't we still doing that?"

"You know what I mean." Before I blew my cover, I had to get this done. I wasn't meant to be a double spy. I was never meant to be any kind of spy.

"Vincent is in the study."

"With your parents?" I slowed my pace as the dread coursed through me.

"No, he's with Rocco. My parents are in Florida."

"Oh." Now this visit didn't seem as daunting. Still as scary as fuck, but at least I didn't have to lie to my aunt and uncle too. "A vacation?"

"More like business." He knocked on the study door. "Lu is here."

"Come in," Vincent said.

When we entered Rocco was there too, sitting by the window. Vincent was behind my uncle's desk, and for the first time I saw a younger version of his father in his features. How had I never noticed before?

"Lu." Rocco stood and hugged me. "How are you?"

"I'm well." I gave him an uneasy smile.

"You look tense," Vincent said.

"Of course she's tense." Sandro sat on the sofa across from the desk. "She's married to Bilotti. Wouldn't you be tense if you had to sleep in the same bed with such a heartless man?"

"I told you it's not that bad." I joined Sandro on the sofa.

"Really?" Rocco sat back down. "I can't see how it isn't absolutely awful."

"Lu is great." Vincent looked at me. "Aren't you?"

Define great.

"I brought this for you." I leaned over and slid the file Romero had given me across the desk. "I hope it's useful."

He opened it and studied the papers as Rocco and Sandro stared at me. I tried to relax and look like I wanted to be there. I failed.

"Sandro said your parents are away." I made light conversation so it would feel less awkward.

"They went to Florida for a getaway," Rocco said.

Sandro said it was business, but I couldn't press

the subject. Romero told me not to ask too many questions.

"Romero has been distracted lately," I offered. "I try to stay out of sight, but I listen when he's with Gio." *Please buy this.* "They are upset about Arturo."

Rocco glanced at Vincent as Vincent looked up from the file.

"What does he say about Arturo?" Vincent asked.

"They have no idea why someone would kill him and dump his body without any explanation." *They know it was you.*

"They don't suspect who is responsible?" Vincent placed the file on his desk.

Of course they do, you idiot. That's how I ended up working against you. If my family hadn't dumped the body at Romero's safe house, my husband might not have figured out I was the snitch.

"They haven't said," I lied.

"Good." Vincent nodded his head. "This information is good, Lu."

"Thank you." My stomach churned when I thought about how comfortable they all were to have me in the enemy's den. Sleeping with him, letting him touch me, and have sex with me whenever he wanted. I didn't mind having sex with Romero, but my cousins didn't know that. They made me do it anyway.

"How much longer is Lu going to do this?" Sandro asked.

"Alessandro." Rocco raised his voice. "Not now."

"Why not now?" Sandro asked. "She has done everything you've asked of her. She's been there long enough. Romero's not stupid. If you keep provoking him, he's going to figure out what she's up to."

"It's okay, Sandro," I said.

"Lu, I know you think you like him, but he won't think twice about killing you." Sandro patted my leg. "We need an exit plan. This was never meant to be a permanent situation."

"Sandro might be right," Rocco agreed.

"She's done when I say she's done," Vincent snapped.

"You mean when Dad says she's done?" Sandro challenged.

"It's the same thing," Vincent said.

"Since when?" Sandro stood and paced the study. "She's not safe."

Sandro's observation unsettled me. What changed his mind? I'd been with Romero for two months. Sandro seemed fine with this set-up. Why did he want me out now?

"Lu." Vincent's loud voice pulled my attention away from Sandro. "You're in no more danger now than you were when you agreed to this. If anything, you've probably gained Romero's trust by now."

You couldn't be more wrong.

"My mother thinks he's fallen for you." Vincent shrugged. "I don't know if that's a good thing for you or not. Being his obsession might not end well when we get you away from him."

"What?" *Get me away from Romero?*

"We never said you had to do this forever," Vincent said. "I need you to do exactly what you're doing, but I promise, when things get dangerous, I will get you out."

"That's reassuring." Rocco gazed out the window.

"Thanks for the information," Vincent said. "I have some calls to make."

"Okay." I stood. "You'll be in touch?"

"Yes." Vincent smiled at me. "

You confirmed mine.

Sandro rose and headed for the door.

I gave Rocco a quick wave before following Sandro out of the study and down the hall.

"Do you want to stay for lunch?" Sandro asked.

"They are calling for a severe storm this afternoon." I pointed to the window. "I think I better go home."

"Another time then."

"Is everything okay?" I asked as we made our way to the foyer. "There was a strange vibe in there."

"I don't know."

"What does that mean?"

"Something big is brewing. I can feel it but

Vincent and dad are so secretive." He sat on the bottom step of the staircase. "More than usual. He and mom ran off to Florida with no warning."

"Do you think it involves Romero?"

"I think so."

"You don't think they're going to—"

"Put a hit on him?" He shook his head. "I don't know what they want with Romero. He's an arms dealer. He's not trying to take over anyone's territory. I don't know why they went after him in the first place."

"I've been wondering that myself." I rested my hand on the banister. "I wish there were a way out of this for both of us."

"Me too."

"Do you really mean that?" I thought about Carson's offer. "You've always been so loyal to your family."

"It's been weird ever since they made you marry Romero. Vincent is running a lot more of the illegal businesses these days. Rocco is indifferent."

"And your parents?"

"I can't read them. My dad always ran the show, or at least I thought he did. Now my mother is more involved." He stretched his legs out. "I don't know what's happening, but I have a weird feeling."

"Do you think it's safe here?"

"Of course." He nodded. "You don't have

anything to be worried about. I'm just overthinking things."

"When did you overthink anything?"

"Ah, probably never, so ignore me." He winked. "How are things really with you and the barbarian? Last time I saw you, you both seemed very content with one another."

That was before he found out I was a traitor.

"Is it a real marriage now?"

"I wouldn't go that far." I gripped the banister. "He's difficult at best. I'm still learning him."

"The way he defended you against mom especially in front of my father, was impressive."

"He has his moments." I glanced at my watch. "I should get going before he sends a search party out for me."

"How did you get away?"

"I'm not a prisoner." *Well, technically I am but he made me come here.* "I can leave the house."

"Lu." Sandro got up and followed me to the door. "Be careful, okay?"

"I'll be fine." I kissed his cheek. "Call me later."

I stepped onto the porch, feeling more unsettled after my conversation with Sandro than I had when I'd first arrived. The wind kicked up and the skies grew darker. This whole visit felt ominous. It was as if the weather knew how chaotic my life was and wanted to enhance it.

"Hey," Sam, my long-time bodyguard, joined me on the porch. "How's my favorite ex-charge?"

"Sam." I hugged him. "I've missed you."

"We didn't even get to say goodbye." He took my hand. "That was hard."

"I know." I had been sad about leaving after the wedding and not talking to him. "That day was strange."

"Strange?"

"I mean that I had to leave. I wasn't really prepared to not have you look after me."

"I knew it was coming when Mr. Torrio announced your engagement to Romero, but I thought there would be more of a transition."

"Me too." I smiled. "I'm still getting used to all the changes."

"Well, married life suits you." He let go of my hand. "You look lovely."

"Thank you." I shot Jag a quick text, telling him I was ready to go. "Are they keeping you busy around here?"

"They find things for me to do." He nodded toward Jag, who was heading up the walkway. "This is your driver?"

"Yes."

"I don't have to frisk him, do I?"

"Please don't."

"Lu." Jag said as he approached, holding an umbrella. "Are you ready?"

They eyed one another. Sam was still protective of me, and Jag wanted to make sure I was okay.

"Jag, this is Sam," I said. "He was my *you* before you. Does that make sense?"

"Nice to meet you, Jag. I hope you're taking care of this special girl." Sam smiled at me. "She was under my protection for many years."

"I'm doing my best." Jag motioned toward me. "Romero is looking for you."

"I'm not surprised." I moved under Jag's umbrella. "It was good seeing you, Sam."

"Take care of yourself." He waved as Jag and I walked to the car.

I'm trying.

Jag opened the back passenger-side door.

"Isn't it silly I don't sit up front?" I slid into the back seat because this was protocol, no matter who my driver slash guard was.

"I never really thought about it." Jag got into the driver's seat. "You sit in the back and I drive."

"What is Jag short for?" I asked.

"It's nothing that mysterious."

"Tell me."

"It's my initials." He glanced at me in the rearview mirror. "My name is John Anthony Genero."

"Oh." Well, that wasn't as eventful as I'd thought.

"Told you it wasn't that mysterious." He laughed. "When I became a bouncer a few years ago at this rough nightclub, Jag sounded cooler, so I went with it."

"You were a bouncer?" The rain pelted against the windows, making it difficult to see the road as we drove from the Torrio estate.

"That's where Gio found me," he said. "I did him a favor, and he got me the job on the security detail. I did a lot of odds and ends for Romero before he decided to trust me with you. I ran errands and… well, whatever he needed."

"Do you like working for my husband?"

"Sure." He turned on to the back road that would eventually lead us to the house. "Wow, this road flooded fast." He turned up the speed on the wipers. "Romero's a tough boss, but he's fair and he pays well. He makes sure our families are well-cared for too."

"Was it always a dream of yours to work for a kingpin?" I giggled. "Was that an entry in your yearbook?"

"Not at all." He smirked. "Did you dream of becoming the wife of such a prominent member of this particular community?"

"That's an interesting way of putting it."

"Well? Were you voted most likely to marry the mob?"

"I think you know enough about my relationship with Romero to know that I had little say in our marriage arrangement. I did what I was told to do."

"Do you regret that?"

I pondered his question for a few minutes. Did I regret marrying Romero? Did I regret falling in love with him? Did I regret what my family made me do? Will I regret what my husband was making me do?

"Fuck!" Jag yelled. A large truck veered into our lane. He swerved to avoid the truck, side-swiping a guardrail. We skidded off the road.

As we crashed through the guardrail that blocked the river, I had only one thought.

I will never regret falling in love with Romero.

CHAPTER 10

Romero

I put my phone on speaker as Gio spoke on the other end. I couldn't sit at my desk any more. Luciana had been gone longer than I had expected and now neither she nor Jag were answering my calls.

"I'm sure she's fine," Gio said. "She hasn't been gone that long."

"Then why isn't she answering my calls?" I shouted. "Jag too. I'm going to kill that son of a bitch. He knows better than to ignore me."

"He wouldn't let anything happen to her," Gio reassured me. "I've seen him with her."

"What the fuck is that supposed to mean?"

"It means he takes his job seriously. He knows she's precious cargo. He also knows you'll kill him if anything happens to her."

"Then why the fuck isn't he here with her right now?"

"Do you want me to send someone to the Torrios or I can access the tracker on the car and get a location?" Gio sighed. "I don't think they are going to hurt her, but if it will ease your mind, I'll do it."

"You know what would ease my mind?" I yelled. "If my wife was home."

"Then maybe you shouldn't have sent her to the enemy camp with phony documents. That might have been the better option."

"Fuck you." What choice did I have? We were under attack and by using Luciana we had a chance at salvaging the damage the Torrios had already set in motion.

"Romero, you need to get your head back in this game. We're no closer to figuring out why they killed Arturo or sent us that message. You are far too distracted and that's going to get us all killed."

"You're right, but if the Torrios take the bait, we'll be in a better position than we were." I'd sent Luciana to see her family with phony shipment dates and locations because I needed to see what they would do with that information. "We'll know in a few days if our plan worked."

"I hope it works and we can forget about the idea of making Lu a spy."

"I didn't turn her into a spy, remember?" I

slammed my hand against my desk. "Her asshole family did that."

"You're going to have to let that go if you want to keep her as your wife."

If I could let it go, I would have. But forgiveness wasn't my strong suit. I glanced out the window, squinting through the pounding rain at two figures at the bottom of the driveway.

"That's still want you want, right? You want to still be married to her?"

Gio kept talking, but I'd lost focus of our conversation when I realized it was Jag and he was carrying Luciana in his arms.

"What the hell?" I sucked in a breath.

"Romero, are you listening?" Gio asked.

"No, I have to go." I grabbed my phone from the desk and ended the call as I hurried down the hallway to the foyer.

In those seconds, all I could think about was her being hurt. What had her family done to her? Was it one of my enemies? Had she been shot? Stabbed? The possibility of something happening to her terrified me. I didn't know how much until right now.

I tugged open the door as Jag brought Luciana up the steps and into the house. Their wet and muddy clothes stuck to their skin. Luciana's teeth chattered as she clung to Jag.

"What the hell happened?" I widened the door so he could get her out of the rain. "Are you okay?"

"I'm fine." She tapped Jag's shoulder. "You can put me down."

"Give her to me." I extended my arms. "And tell me what happened."

"I can stand on my own," Luciana insisted.

Both of us ignored her as Jag handed her over. I needed to see for myself that she was okay. Feel her in my arms and press her against me for warmth.

"It was raining heavily," Jag said. "An oncoming car veered into our lane, so I swerved to miss it and ended up in a ditch a few minutes from here. The car is still there."

"Are you hurt?" I asked Luciana.

"Just my pride." She smiled in embarrassment. "I slipped and fell in the ditch when we were trying to get out of the car."

"Isn't it your job to keep her from falling in a ditch?" I knelt in front of her and reached for her wet shoe as I continued to berate her incompetent guard. "Isn't that why I pay you?"

Why hadn't I put a tracker on her phone? I'd be rectifying that today.

"I'm sorry, boss," Jag said. "It all happened so fast."

"It wasn't his fault, and he made sure we didn't get killed by the car that came into our lane." Luciana shivered. "It's okay."

"No, it isn't." I stood and shoved Jag against the

wall. "I trusted you with my wife and now look at her."

I dropped to my knees again, too wild with anger to think straight. I finished removing her other shoe and sopping wet socks because concentrating on her put me in control.

"I'm really sorry," Jag said again.

"Go figure out the car situation." I needed him out of my sight before I broke his jaw. "The service will probably call Gio," I said. "Make sure he knows everyone is all right."

"Okay." He lingered for a moment, staring at Luciana.

"Go!" I pointed toward the door.

"This wasn't his fault." Luciana wiped the drops of water that dripped out of her hair and trickled down her face.

"We're going to have to disagree on that."

"I'm freezing." She rubbed her hands along her arms." I have to get out of these clothes."

"Come on." I lifted her in my arms and carried her to the stairs.

"Where are we going?" She hung on to me, trying to steal my body heat, but it wasn't working. She trembled the whole time I climbed the steps.

"I'm getting you into a hot shower."

"I can do that myself," she argued. "You don't have to help me."

I took her to the master bathroom and shut the

door before setting her on her feet. Turning on the water, I closed the shower door and joined her in the corner of the room. I looked her over, making sure she was okay.

"I told you I'm fine. You don't need to hover." When I unbuttoned her shirt and peeled it from her cold, damp skin, she shivered. I ran the back of my hand down her neck and between her breasts, popping the clasp at the front of her bra. I couldn't stop myself from ogling her nipples as they peaked and tempted me. I tossed the pink lace on top of her shirt and then dragged my fingers down her stomach. She dropped her gaze when I undid the button on her jeans and lowered the zipper.

After I tugged her pants down, I turned her to investigate the red mark on her upper thigh. When I smoothed my palm over it, she wiggled away.

"That's going to bruise." I stared at her in the mirror. "Does it hurt?"

"A little." She smiled. "I bruised my ego more. Jag wanted to lift me out of the car, but I insisted I could do it myself."

"Of course you did." I turned her back to face me. "Next time, let him help you."

"I hope there isn't a next time." She held onto my arm as I glided her panties over her hips. "One near-death experience is enough."

"One?" I snickered. "I've lost count of how many times I've almost died."

"That's not funny."

"Not when it's your life, it isn't." The steam escaped from the stall when I opened the shower door. "Get in."

"I got your shirt all wet."

I looked down at my dirt smeared shirt.

"You can join me." The uncertainty in her expression took me by surprise. "If you want."

You're afraid I'll turn you down.

"Is that what you want?" I asked.

"Yes," she answered without hesitation.

As she entered the stall, I undressed, debating how I wanted this to play out. I could offer her comfort and take care of her after her accident that could have been much worse. Going to her family today deposited plenty of anxiety on her. Maybe she just needed to be close to me. Needed to know that I could be tender.

When I joined her under the hot stream of the multiple shower heads, taking in the beauty of her naked form, my dick had other ideas, and they had nothing to do with being caring or gentle. I pulled her close, brushing my erection between her thighs.

"I did what you told me." She ran her delicate fingers across my lips. "I gave Vincent the information."

Did she want to cash in on her efforts?

"Did your family believe you?"

"They have no reason to doubt me."

"Who was there?" I pushed the hair from her face, catching a few strands between my fingers.

"My cousins." She trailed her hand down my chest. "Vincent was very interested in the file. Rocco didn't have much to say, but Sandro was off."

"What do you mean?" I circled my finger around her nipple. "Did he suspect something?"

"No, he said things were different around the house. Vincent was handling more of the business."

That was true. The oldest Torrio sibling had more of a presence lately.

"My aunt and uncle are in Florida."

"What are they doing there?"

"Sandro said it was business, but Rocco said it was a vacation." She inched closer to me. "I couldn't figure out what they were doing there."

"Hmm." I wrapped my arms around her waist and brought her to me, closing any space between us. "That's useful information."

Carlos Garcia, one of my associates and a well-known member of a large cartel, had been spotted in a nightclub in Miami a few days ago. If Antonio was in Florida on business, I'd bet my fortune he was there to see Garcia.

"I did good?" She bit her lip.

"You did real good, baby." I backed her against the wall, leaning down and kissing her for a few moments. "What do you want in return?"

She glanced down between us, eyeing my aroused cock.

Yes, we both know what I want. What I'm about to take.

"Don't be shy." I took her chin between my fingers and forced her to look into my eyes. "Tell me what you want."

"I want you."

"You're going to have to be more specific." The sexual tension swirled between us thicker than the steam. "I want you to tell me what you want. When you have your hand in your panties in the middle of the night, what am I doing to you?"

"Fucking me." She sucked in a breath.

"How do I fuck you?"

When I lifted her up, she locked her legs around my hips.

"Fast and hard."

"My favorite way." I shoved my pelvis forward, slammed her against the wall, and entered her with one quick thrust.

Her arms fell from my shoulders as I pounded into her. She gripped my biceps, trying to hold herself up, but it wasn't necessary. I had her.

"You've been such a bad girl." I squeezed her backside in my firm hold. "And bad girls get fucked hard."

"Yes." She tightened her grip with her legs, clenching around my shaft.

"But you know what's even better?"

She shook her head, keeping her eyes shut as I continued my relentless assault on her pussy.

"When an obedient little brat does what I tell her to do." I kissed her neck, biting her soft flesh. "Are you going to be a good girl and do what I say?"

"Yes."

"If you do, you get my cock."

"I want that," she moaned.

"I know you do."

I pressed my lips to hers, kissing her deep, probing my tongue inside her mouth as I continued my quick tempo between her legs. My muscles tightened and my veins stretched beneath my skin as my balls ached for release.

"Romero, I'm..."

When she screamed my name, I couldn't hold on any longer. I lifted her arms above her head, slowed my pace and shot my load deep into her core, claiming her once again.

"Oh..." she cried out as she thrashed against me.

I moved in and out of her until she settled from her climax. She opened her eyes when I placed her on her feet, steadying her between the wall and my body. I took her face between my hands and kissed her slowly, savoring the connection.

I wanted more than anything to tell her what she meant to me. How scared I was when I saw Jag carrying her up the driveway. But all I could do was kiss her. That was the only way I could express myself for now.

"You did good today," I whispered.

"Can you forgive me?"

The vulnerability in her voice gutted me, but I answered as truthfully as I could.

"I don't know."

CHAPTER 11

Luciana

It had been a week since the visit with my family. My conversation with Sandro left me worried about him. I'd never seen my cousin so at odds with his way of life. He was always resigned to it. He accepted it for what it was and went on living. My cousin liked his status and the privileges that came with it.

I hadn't seen much of Romero since our shower escapade. If he wasn't in his study with the door shut, he was at one of his new clubs. I only knew about the clubs because pictures of him tended to show up on social media. There were plenty of women who were obsessed with the whereabouts of my husband. I even found three social media pages dedicated to him. Didn't people have anything better to do?

"Lu?" Stella's voice brought me back to the present. "Are you listening?"

"Huh?" My cheeks burned when I realized she had been talking to me and I hadn't responded.

"Are we still making these cookies?"

"Yes." I nodded.

"Are you sure you're up for it?"

"I guess I was lost in thought. Sorry."

"That happens to you a lot." She preheated the oven for the chocolate cookies she was teaching me to bake. "You have so much on your young mind. It must be hard dealing with the things that go on around here."

Stella was like everyone else Romero employed at the house. They all knew who he was and what he did for a living. They wouldn't be employed here if he couldn't trust them. Not having to hide from her made talking to her easier.

"I try to stay out of the things that go on around here." *Although, I'm not very successful.* "Should I beat the eggs, butter, and sugar?"

"Yes." She placed the silver bowl in front of me. "Set it in the mixer stand and put it on low."

"I like having you around." Having Stella in the house was an unexpected comfort. For the first time in my life, I had a friend.

I turned on the fancy black mixer that matched the rest of the appliances in the kitchen. Romero must have hired someone when he bought the house to stock it with top-of-the-line everything. I didn't know what half of the items were for.

"It's nice being around." She placed flour and some other dry ingredients into another mixing bowl. "I miss my kids not being in the house, so being here with you helps."

I imagined her baking cookies with her three girls. The older two were twins and the younger one was just two years younger than her siblings. Stella had her hands full when they were little, but from the looks of her, she handled motherhood with ease.

"You're not that much older than my twins, but I can't see either of them being married anytime soon." She brought over her mixing bowl. "You can start adding this to your bowl."

"I didn't see myself being married either." I began pouring the additional ingredients into the bowl.

"How did that come about?"

"Circumstances, I guess." I peered into the bowl, noticing the mixture was forming into dough.

"Are you happy with the circumstances?"

"I, um, was adjusting to them, but then things changed. Things beyond my control, and now I don't know how to fix them, but I'm trying."

"Do you want to fix them?"

"I do, but I don't know if Romero does."

"Have you asked him?"

My heart sunk into my gut at the thought of asking Romero if he could forgive me again.

"He's not ready for that conversation." He was avoiding me since I had asked him if he could forgive me. I didn't know why I had asked him.

"That looks about ready." She pointed to the batter before handing me the chocolate chips. "You can stir these in with a spoon."

"Okay." I opened the bag and sprinkled the chocolate chips into the batter.

"I know he isn't the easiest man to communicate with." She washed some of the dirty bowls and utensils. "You should have met his father."

I pondered her words as the water splashed in the sink.

"I don't need anymore overbearing, scary men in my life." I rolled my eyes. "Between my uncles, cousins, husband, brother-in-law, guards, and FBI agents, well, I've had about enough."

"Ah, Lu, is there anything I could do to make your life a little easier?"

"You're doing it." I motioned toward the cookie dough. "My mother died when I was young. I've never really had a stable family life. My aunt and uncle did the bare minimum for me. I had every luxury you could imagine, but I didn't have much emotional support."

"It must have been a very lonely life."

"It still is." I didn't regret admitting that, but I regretted it was true.

"I'm sorry."

"You don't have to be. I'm fine."

"You say that a lot." She shook her head. "I like Romero. I've known him for a long time, but if one of my daughters wanted to date him, I'd tell them to run in the opposite direction."

"Believe me, I wanted to run." I giggled. "But that was before I got to know him. He can be kind and generous when he doesn't feel threatened."

"I can see how much you love him."

"We were getting there before I..." Even if she knew about Romero's occupation, I wasn't ready to admit what I had done to him. "It's complicated."

"Isn't it always with a man like Romero?" She dried her hands and joined me at the island. "If Romero is who you want, then you should do everything you can to make this work."

"I'm trying."

"But now I'm going to offer you some motherly advice." She smiled at me. "For any relationship to work, you have to find out who you are. I don't think you've had a chance to do that yet. I'm just making observations, but you're young and naïve, and I have a feeling your family had plenty to do with marrying you off to Romero."

"Your observations are spot on."

"I'm not saying you and Romero can't work, but you have to find your voice and make your husband hear it. Otherwise, you won't have much of a marriage."

"Thank you." I heard every word, but I had to figure out a way to make Romero see who I really was.

"Let's finish these cookies."

"What do we do next?"

"We drop the dough onto the baking sheets." She handed me a spoon. "Scoop some out and plop it on the sheet. Make sure you have fun with it."

"Like this?" I scooped out the dough, but it stuck to the spoon. "Why isn't it coming off?" I laughed. "Did I screw it up?"

"Not at all." She grinned. "You're doing great."

"If you say so."

"Do you know why Romero is going to love these cookies?"

"Because he likes chocolate chips?"

"Because you made them for him."

She pulled up a stool and sat at the center island next to me. Grabbing a spoon, she started her own tray.

"A man can forgive almost anything when you bake him cookies." She patted my hand. "Trust me."

"I hope you're right."

Later that evening, I went into the kitchen and put some cookies on a plate. Romero didn't make it home for dinner, but I heard him come in and shower in the master bathroom. I assumed he was going out again tonight.

I treaded down the hall quietly, not sure what I thought I would accomplish in my black boy shorts and tight matching tank top. I wanted my husband to notice me. To make an effort. When would he give me a sign that he wanted this relationship?

I peeked into the office through the ajar door. The dimly lit room was quiet, but I spied Romero sitting in the chair by the window drinking a glass of vodka. He wore a black suit with a crisp white dress shirt. Omitting a tie, he left the first couple buttons of his shirt undone, revealing the top of his tattoo. A silver watch that I'd never seen him wear before adorned his wrist. It probably cost more than some people's cars.

He was far too sexy to leave the house without me on his arm. I wondered if his wedding band even deterred anyone from trying to sleep with him. I wondered if *he* tried to deter anyone from sleeping with him. I wanted to believe he wouldn't cheat on me, but it was difficult when we didn't communicate.

He was lost in thought, but there was a peacefulness surrounding him. I turned away from the door because I decided disturbing him with my silly cookies was a ridiculous idea.

"Where are you going?" His voice cut through me, halting me from taking another step. "Come here."

I hesitated, but then realized there was nowhere for me to run. When I entered the room, he brought the glass to his lips and took a long sip, keeping his gaze fixated on me.

"What brings you down here at this time of the night?"

"I made these for you." I set the cookies on his desk.

"You made cookies?"

"Stella taught me how."

"Nice." He motioned over my body with his hand. "Are you going to bed?"

"I was going to watch a movie." I rocked back on my heels. "Do you want to join me?"

"Sorry, butterfly, but I have to go to the club and check on some stuff."

"That's the third time this week." The stab of his rejection hurt more than I thought it would.

"Are you keeping tabs on me?"

"Like you're keeping tabs on me now?" She shook her head. "No, I'm not."

"Are you referring to the phone tracking app I had Gio install on your phone?" He set his glass on the floor by the chair. "I should have done that as soon as we were engaged. I figured having a guard on you was enough, but after what happened the other day, I saw the need to know where you are at all times. It's for your protection and my sanity."

"Well, no one wants you to go insane."

"Thank you for not fighting Gio on it."

"I didn't think I had a choice."

"You didn't." He smirked. "But since you willingly handed over your phone for him to install the app, he didn't have to get me involved."

"Can I track you?"

"No."

"What if I need to know where you are?" It only seemed fair. "You have been out a lot lately."

"Business calls to me. Taking over three new clubs in a busy city requires much attention." He extended his hand. "Come sit with me."

After I took his hand, he moved me into his lap, facing me away from him so that my back was against his chest. He buried his face in my hair and inhaled deeply.

"You smell good." He ran his hand along my thigh and over my hip, igniting a flame inside my stomach. "The things I could do to you." He kissed my neck. "Maybe later."

"You could stay with me and do whatever you want." I spread my legs in an embarrassing attempt to keep him here. "Don't go."

"Where's this bold side coming from?" He slithered his hand under my tank top and to my breasts. "I'm not complaining."

"Maybe I just want you to stay."

"I wish I could." He swirled his finger around my nipple. "I've been making some changes at the clubs and overseeing some shipments. My presence is required tonight."

"Well, I'll let you go." When I tried to get off his lap, he pulled me back down and turned me to face him. "I don't want you to be upset with me."

"I'm not."

"You're lying." He took my chin between his fingers. "Don't lie to me anymore. I thought I made it abundantly clear that I don't like it."

"I..." The intensity in his expression frightened me, but it also commanded me to say what he needed from me. "I want you to stay, but I understand why you can't."

"That's better." He brought his lips to mine and kissed me, keeping a firm grip on my chin as he ran his other hand through my hair. "You should go or I'll be late."

"Okay." Disappointment filled my soul. "Be safe tonight."

"Always." He kissed me softly. "Enjoy your movie."

"I will."

I slipped off his lap, but he grabbed my hand. I glanced over my shoulder and waited for him to speak. There was a struggle in his eyes. He was always so sure of himself, but I didn't see his confidence. He seemed conflicted, and that affected me more than I had expected.

"Luciana, it may not seem like it, but I am trying to get over what your family did to us."

My family? He didn't say what I did to him. That was progress.

"It's going to take me time to get there and I want you... I need you to give me that time."

I leaned down and kissed his cheek because he had no idea that was what I needed him to say. I needed to see his uncertainty. From the moment we met, he displayed strength and authority. It was easy to see him as uncaring and without feelings, but that wasn't who he was. He was so much more and I wanted to know the real him. The side he hid from the rest of the world. The part he could only show me.

"I'll be patient."

"That's my girl." When he winked at me, it was the first time in weeks I had felt any hope that we could salvage this relationship. "Thanks for the cookies."

Was Stella right? Could a man forgive anything when a woman baked him cookies?

I needed a mafia wife's handbook.

CHAPTER 12

*R*omero

"Is everything in place with that shipment?" I asked Gio as we walked down the hall from my study. "It has to be on time and no surprises."

"It's scheduled for dock twenty-seven." He glanced at his watch. "I don't anticipate any problems."

"Good."

As we continued down the hall, I saw a group of my guards staring out at the pool through the sunroom windows.

"What's this?" I asked.

"We're having a quick meeting," Gio said.

"What's got them so intrigued?"

When I joined them in the sunroom, they dispersed from the window. No one looked at me but they nodded and cleared their throats. It was as if they were guilty and they knew it.

"What's going on?" I asked.

"Nothing," Salvi said. "We're just waiting for Gio."

"Really." I shoved him out of the way to see what had them so distracted. Luciana stepped into the pool wearing a pale blue string bikini. I couldn't even be mad at her for wearing it. I bought the frigging bathing suit for her and she looked spectacular in it.

I turned so fast, they all backed away from me, but not before I grabbed Joey, my head of security, by the throat. "Are you fucking kidding me? Do you think I pay you to stalk my wife?"

"No, of course not," he said. "We were just... well, she's..."

"She's what?" I shouted.

"Beautiful," he admitted.

"Where the fuck is Jag? Why isn't he protecting her from you lowlives?"

"He needed a few hours off today," Gio said. "He'll be back tonight."

"Get back to work." I pushed Joey into the other three idiots standing behind him. "Before I shoot all of you."

"Sorry," one of them mumbled.

"You will be if it happens again." I tossed over my

shoulder before I opened the patio doors. "You're all replaceable, don't forget that."

They apologized to Gio as I shut the doors and made my way down the path to the pool. As disrespectful as my guards were, I couldn't blame them. Luciana could make any man lose all sense. Look what she had done to me. No one had ever dared to betray me the way she had, but yet here she was, living in my house, using my last name, and swimming in my pool. Baking me fucking cookies and making me admit I needed time. Why the hell had I told her that? Because with one vulnerable look from her, she stopped me dead in my tracks. I wanted to give her anything her heart desired.

When she spotted me, she swam to the edge of the pool and rested her arms on the side. The sunlight bounced off the water and streamed around her. Water dripped off her hair and down her neck to her breasts. I couldn't think of one swimsuit model who had anything on her.

And she was all mine.

"You're home," she said.

"I do live here."

"I wasn't sure." She teased me. "Why don't you change into your bathing suit and join me?" She pushed off the wall and swam on her back. "The water is perfect."

Not as perfect as you.

I glanced over at the table under the cabana and

saw a stack of books. I looked through them, noting they all had a law or criminal justice theme.

She got out of the pool and joined me under the cabana.

"Where did these come from?" I asked.

"Jag took me to the library this morning before he left."

I took a towel off the lounge chair and spread it open for her.

"I can air dry."

"No, you can't." I motioned for her to come closer so I could wrap her in the towel. "You had an audience. They are lucky I didn't kill all of them for watching you out here."

"Isn't it their job to watch me?"

"Not when you're almost naked."

"Well, it seems like that's a *you* problem. I should be able to go for a swim in my own backyard without a bunch of guards watching me."

"You're absolutely right." I draped her in the towel. "It's not going to happen again."

"So, then, I don't need this." She shrugged out of the towel and let it fall to her feet. "Since you have it all under control."

"You look fantastic in the bikini." I took in her flawless skin, sexy breasts, and flat stomach. "I don't think you'll be wearing it much longer, though."

She took a bottle of water out of the mini-fridge and opened the cap.

"The books." I pointed to the pile on the table. "I thought we discussed this."

"You said I couldn't go back to school." She sipped the water, wrapping her lips around the rim and making me think about what she could do to me right now. "You didn't say I couldn't go to the library and educate myself."

"This school thing means a lot to you, doesn't it?" I took a seat at the table. "Do you want to be a lawyer because your uncle said you couldn't, or is it something you really want for yourself?"

"I've never had much for myself," she said. "I've always done what everyone else has told me to do. I wanted to get a four-year degree, but I was told an associate degree would be enough. I wanted to go to law school, but had to settle on being a paralegal instead." She paced around the pool deck. "I don't get to make my own decisions. About anything."

"Were you going to say you didn't want to get married?"

"You know I didn't."

"They made you anyway." I hated she felt trapped, but I was glad her family made her marry me. "Then they made you spy on me."

"And now you're making me betray them." She shrugged. "See, I have nothing for me."

I didn't enjoy hearing her talk this way. *Death would be better than this.* She was lonely and miserable being my wife.

"You didn't answer my question. Why do you want to be a lawyer?"

"My father was a lawyer."

"I knew that."

"When my uncle's sons followed in their father's footsteps, I wondered if my dad would be proud if I wanted to follow in his. The more I wanted it, the further out of reach it became." She stopped pacing and took another sip of water. "When you said you would support me, I finally thought my dream was going to happen. I should have known it wasn't in the cards."

"I was furious with you when I told you I wouldn't let you go back to school." I knew by going back on my word it would hurt her and at the time, I wanted to hurt her the way she had wounded me. "I didn't know you were trying to honor your late father."

"It doesn't matter." When she gave me a fake smile, I saw the broken woman that always had to put up a brave front when everyone around her, including me, told her the way things had to be. "There are plenty of books in the library and lots of stuff online to keep me busy for now. By the time I'm ready to go back to school, I'm going to be so smart." She laughed, and I realized she was covering up her disappointment again. "I'm young. I'll get there, eventually."

How doesn't she hate me?

"Are you going out again tonight?"

"Probably, I might have some things that need my attention."

"You might, or you do?"

"Can we go back to the college situation again?"

"I don't have anything else to say about it." She pushed her sunglasses on top of her head. "It is what it is. I've accepted it and want to move on unless you're going to tell me I can't go back to the library."

"I have something to say about it, and I want you to hear it." I motioned her to come to me. "Sit with me."

"I'll get your pants wet."

"Do I look like I care?" I tugged her into my lap and rested my hand on her thigh. "I want you to enroll in the fall semester."

She gazed out at the pool, but didn't say anything as she pressed her lips together.

"Did you hear what I said?"

She nodded.

"I thought you would be more excited."

"Thanks for the offer, but I'm going to pass."

"You're going to pass?" *What the fuck?* "Why?"

"Have you ever heard the saying fool me once?"

"I'm not trying to trick you."

"No, but if you get mad at me or I do something wrong, you'll pull back the offer and I'll be broken again." She picked up a book from the stack and placed it in front of her. "I'll stick to the library books."

"You're an impossible woman. One that I may never understand." I turned her to face me. "Are you planning on screwing me over again?"

"You know I'm not." She looked into my eyes. "Don't you?"

I'm trying, baby.

"Romero, I won't betray you again."

"I want you to go back to school." I took her hand in mine. "I promise I won't hold this over your head. I won't go back on my word again. Do whatever you need to do to start classes in the fall and I'll pay the bill. You honor your father, understand?"

"I don't know what to say."

"Say yes and don't argue with me."

"You're being serious?" Her eyes filled with tears. "You're going to let me do this?"

"If it's what you want, I want it for you." I wiped the tears that escaped from her eyes. "I'm sorry I took it away from you."

"Thank you." More tears slid down her cheeks. "I feel like I really need this."

I wrapped my arms around her and held her to my chest as she cried against me. I wanted to make her happy with my offer, but it seemed as if all I did was cause her more anxiety.

"I didn't mean to make you cry."

"It's okay." She clung to me. "It's been a tough

couple of weeks. I need to find a rhythm and a routine. I want a normal life."

"Don't we all?" I laughed into her hair. "Now you have something to focus on."

"I'd like to focus on us." She kissed along my jaw until she found my lips. "Can we do that?"

"I'm always ready to focus on you." I positioned her so that her legs were on either side of my hips. "Where would you like me to focus first?"

When her cheeks turned red, I knew what her answer was.

"My dirty girl." I gripped her hips and thrusted her forward, running my tongue along the top of her breasts. "Do you want me to fuck you?"

"Right here?"

"Normally, I'd say yes." I trailed my hand down her stomach and slipped it inside her bikini bottom. "But since we had an audience earlier, I'm going to have to take you to the bedroom."

"Ah…" She arched her back and pushed into my fingers. "Take me upstairs."

"Let's go." As I scooted her off my lap, I noticed two unexpected guests coming through the back gate. "What the fuck?"

"What?"

"Put your cover up on."

"What? Why?"

"Now," I shouted as I grabbed her bathing suit cover up from the chair. "We have company."

"What is Carter doing here?" She pulled the white mesh dress that barely covered anything over her bikini. It was better than nothing.

"He better not be here to see you." I got up from the chair and stood in front of Luciana. "Agent Morgan, what brings you here?" I glanced over his shoulder at his partner. "Two of you? What do I owe the honor?"

"Mr. and Mrs. Bilotti," Morgan said. "I see you're enjoying an afternoon by the pool." He looked past me, focusing on my half-naked wife. "Lu, it's good to see you."

"Carter." She moved in front of me and began gathering her books. "I'll leave you to your business."

"No." I took her hand and positioned her next to me. "Stay."

"Is that really wise?" Morgan asked.

"Since you insist on coming to my home without my attorney present, I think it's a good idea for Luciana to stay."

"Whatever you think is best for your wife." He smiled at Luciana. "We're here to bring you into the bureau for some questions."

"For what?" I asked.

"Right now, we have a team of agents descending on dock twenty-seven." He glanced at his phone. "Would you know anything about that?"

"More than you think." I smirked. "What do you know about it?"

"I think you better contact your attorney."

When I glanced down at my ringing phone, I saw it was Gio. *Perfect timing.*

"Hello," I answered. "We have guests."

"The Feds?" Gio asked. "Joey told me he let them through the back gate."

"What does our contact at the dock say?"

"The FBI intercepted the shipment. I'm calling Santino Marchelli after I hang up with you, but I wanted you to know. I'm headed to the docks now."

"Thanks for the information, little brother." I ended the call and placed my phone in my pocket. Luciana took my hand in hers as if she expected a problem, I welcomed her comforting gesture. A united front. Husband and wife. *That's who we are.*

Agent Morgan's lips turned into a satisfied grin as if to say "*Gotcha.*"

"Is something wrong, Mr. Bilotti?"

CHAPTER 13

Luciana

I didn't know what possessed me to take Romero's hand, but it seemed like the right thing to do. Carson gave off a strange vibe, but Romero was as calm as ever. The timing of Gio's call made me anxious. I was certain I was far more worried than my husband was at the moment. Had Romero screwed up and given the Feds something incriminating? Were they here to arrest him?

If he got arrested, what would I do? The thought of them taking him from me frightened me.

"Is something wrong, Mr. Bilotti?" The smugness in Carson's voice made me think he knew something he shouldn't.

"Not at all," Romero said. "As a matter of fact, you might want to make a call to your men on the docks."

"Why is that?" Carson asked.

"Because at the moment, they are seizing a very expensive shipment of vodka." Romero pulled me to his side and placed his arm around my waist. "A legal shipment, I might add, because contrary to what you believe, I'm a legitimate business person."

"Really?" Carson glanced at his partner, who was retrieving his phone from his pocket.

"Now, I can't tell you how to do your job, but I don't see the benefit of you interfering with my shipment. If you destroy it, my insurance will cover the mistake, but you would ruin perfectly good merchandise and waste many people's time. I don't know about the FBI, but I'm too busy for bullshit."

My confident husband seemed to have the upper-hand.

"My brother Gio and my attorney, Santino Marchelli, maybe you've heard of him?" Romero shrugged. "They are on their way to the docks to stop your search and seizure."

"Marchelli? Another mobbed up attorney. He can't stop anything."

"I wouldn't be so sure," Romero said.

Carson's partner stepped away and made a phone call. He rushed to the back gate, but by the way he shouted and gestured, it appeared Romero won this battle.

"I'm sure once your partner, Agent Paulson, is it?" Romero pointed at Carson's partner. "Well, once he gets off the phone you won't have any reason to take me to the bureau. I'm even willing to give you the name of my associate who sold me the vodka. I'll give you a bottle. It's good stuff."

"Nothing but the best for your clubs." The disgust in Cason's voice was apparent.

"Don't waste my time and the taxpayers' money seizing a shipment I have every right to move through those docks." He nodded toward Paulson who was heading toward us. "It won't go well for your career."

"Agent Morgan," Paulson said. "Our business is concluded here. We won't be taking Mr. Bilotti in for questioning."

"Today," Carson said.

"Luciana." Romero took my hand in his. "See what happens when a man *comes* for his suspect too early?" He held me close to his side. "You two can see yourself out. Don't come back here without a warrant or I will file harassment charges."

"You'll get yours, Bilotti." Carson switched his attention to me. "Lu, my offer still stands."

"I told you I don't need your help." As I spoke, Romero dug his fingers into my hip. "Please leave us alone."

The two agents left without another word. Romero stood perfectly still, breathing heavy and holding me tighter than I would have liked. Carson had deliberately provoked Romero, and now I was going to pay the price.

"I'm guessing you got the better of them?" I tried to get his mind off Carson's parting words. "Maybe they will leave you alone now."

"What did he offer you, Luciana?"

"Nothing, it was nothing."

"Just tell me the fucking truth the first time I ask you," he yelled. "Is that so difficult?"

When he shouted, I let go of his hand and backed away.

"Don't." He grabbed my wrist and brought me to him. "What did he mean when he said his offer still stands?"

"The last time he was here, he told me he could help me get away from you if I wanted."

"What did you tell him?" He let go of me and gripped the sides of his head in his hands. "Why does he still think you need him?"

"I told him I didn't need his help. I didn't want to leave."

"Anything else I need to know?"

"He gave me his card with a private number where he could be reached at any time."

"Why didn't you tell me that?" His jaw tightened once he heard my admission. That was never a good sign.

"I don't know." I looked down. "I was afraid you would be upset. You were already so mad at me. I didn't want to add fuel to the fire."

"I am upset."

"I threw the card away." I tore it up into tiny pieces and flushed it down the toilet so Romero couldn't find it and go after the federal agent for giving it to me. I was trying to protect my erratic husband. "I didn't need it and I didn't think it was important for you to know."

"Don't you get it?" He reached for me, taking my wrists in his hands. "Anything that concerns you concerns me."

"I understand."

"No." He squeezed my wrists. "I don't think you do, but you're going to learn."

He took me by the arm and led me in the direction of the house.

"Where are we going?"

"I'm going to teach you a lesson so you'll never keep something from me again."

He opened the sliders that led to the kitchen and pulled me inside. We headed up the back staircase and down the hallway to the master bedroom. Stella wasn't here today, so she didn't have to witness my barbaric husband dragging me through the house. I had to admit, I was more aroused than afraid. What did that say about me?

He brought me into his room and dropped me on the couch in the sitting area. My heartbeat strummed loudly between my ears as my chest heaved.

"I don't understand why you can't be honest with

me." He removed his gun from the back of his pants and set it on the top of the armoire. "Don't I deserve the truth from you?"

"I didn't lie to you, I just…"

"Withheld the truth," he shouted.

"Please stop yelling."

He took off his watch and placed it next to his gun before undoing his tie and unbuttoning his shirt.

"I specifically asked you what Morgan was doing here that day, and you told me you didn't know."

"I didn't know."

"He was here to check on you." He tugged his shirt from his pants and removed it, leaving his tie draped around his neck before taking off his shoes and socks. "Why do you suppose he did that?"

I didn't have the answer he was looking for so I stayed quiet.

When he came closer to me, I gaped at his bare torso covered in the glorious ink that accentuated every muscle on his chest and abs. I wanted to wrap myself around him and let him take control of my body. Let him take control of me.

"Do you think he wants what's mine?" He yanked me from the sofa and tugged the cover-up over my head. "Does he want to protect you from me?"

"I don't need his protection." I traced my finger along his chest. "I only need you."

"Are you sure?" He undid the knot at the base of

my neck, causing my bikini top to fall below my breasts. "Are you sure you don't see him as a way out?"

"Yes." Didn't he understand I didn't want to be rescued from him?

He reached around my back and tugged on the strap, allowing the top to drop to my feet. Licking his lips, he lowered his mouth to my nipple, and then swirled his tongue around it. I ran my hands along his arms, smoothing my palms over his biceps and up to his shoulders.

In the mirror across the room, I watched his back muscles flex as he licked and sucked my nipples. Never abandoning his attention to my breasts, he moved his hands to my waist and slipped my bikini bottoms down my legs. They pooled around my ankles. When I stepped out of them, my thigh grazed his erection, pushing against his pants.

"What should I do with you?" He inched back and took in my naked form. "So many possibilities."

I bit my bottom lip as he pondered his question. My insides pulsed with desire and my body hummed.

"Let's start by restraining you." He slipped the tie from his neck and turned me around so that I faced away from him. "I like having you at my mercy."

He secured my hands behind my back, tying the knot tight enough so that I couldn't wiggle out of it. Not that I would dare.

"Get on your knees." He guided me down in front of the sofa. "I like the view."

He unbuckled his belt and snapped it through the loops, placing it on the sofa beside my face.

"I'll be using that later." He dropped to his knees and settled behind me. "But first, let's get you good and ready for what I have planned."

His solid chest brushed against my shoulder blades as he reached around and placed his hand over my mound. I arched my back when he slipped his fingers inside me.

"You're so wet," he whispered into my ear. "Are you excited about being taught a lesson?"

"Only if you're the one doing the teaching." I rocked against his hand, forcing him to go deeper.

"That's an excellent answer." He trailed his free hand up my stomach and to my breasts, taking my nipple between his thumb and finger. "Always so ready for me."

He worked me with his fingers, pushing them in and out of my slick sex, rubbing my clit as he squeezed and rolled my nipples. The stimulation was divine. The slow build-up made me quiver against him, agonizing for the payoff.

When he withdrew his fingers, I let out a frustrated breath.

"Oh." He laughed into my hair. "Did you think I was going to let you come?" He trailed his finger to my lips, spreading my juices along them before shoving his fingers inside my mouth. "Suck," he demanded.

I swirled my tongue around his wet fingers, tasting my arousal.

"Such a filthy girl." He turned me around and placed me on my back on the floor. My hands were still bound behind me, but I settled into a somewhat comfortable position. "You shouldn't be the only one who gets a taste."

I gaze up at him as he spread my legs open with his rough hands. The determination in his expression excited me. His shirtless body hovered over me. He'd undone the button on his pants, causing his navy blue boxer briefs to peek out of his waistband. I struggled against the tie around my hands because I wanted to touch him.

"You're not going anywhere." He situated himself between my spread legs. "Don't bother trying."

"I don't want to go anywhere, but can you untie me?"

"No." He slapped the inside of my thigh. "I like when you're restrained." He lifted my leg and rested it on his shoulder. "Be a good girl and let me do what I want."

If letting him do what he wanted meant letting him drive me crazy with his wicked tongue, I could oblige.

"Oh..." I moaned when he slowly licked the length of my slit.

I rocked my head from side to side and tried to loosen the restraints on my hands, but it was no use. I relaxed my legs and focused on the sensation he created between my thighs. His tongue stroked deliberate and long. He paid plenty of attention to my clit, licking and sucking it into his hot, greedy mouth.

A cool sheen of sweat covered my flesh as he added his fingers, working with his mouth. My arousal dripped out of my sex and down my backside. The more he fingered me, the wetter I became. Once again, the sensation in my core shot lower and my legs tightened on his shoulder. I was so close. Too close.

"Romero..."

He flipped me onto my stomach and forced me to my knees before I could climax. I screamed out, but he only laughed at my frustration.

"This is a punishment, remember?" He positioned himself behind me, reaching for the belt he'd left on the sofa. "Do you know why I'm doing this?"

"Because I forgot to tell you something."

"Forgot?" The leather slapped against my ass. I sucked in a breath, the unexpected pain hot against my skin. "Do you want to rephrase that?"

"I didn't tell you something."

"You *deliberately* didn't tell me." He drew his hand back, hitting me harder than before. "Why is that?"

"Because I didn't want to make you mad."

Another hard whack with the belt.

"I was wrong." When he hit me again, I screamed. "I'm sorry."

"That's better." He smoothed his palm against my skin and I jumped. "I like when your ass is red from my belt." He hit me again, this time a little softer.

"I like it too." My body hummed with desire.

"Let's see how much you like it." He pushed his fingers inside me and pumped in and out. "Dirty girl."

"Please..." My overstimulated nerves couldn't take much more.

"Please what?" He drew his hand back and slapped me again with the leather of the belt as he continued to finger me. "Do you want me to keep hitting you?" He brushed the belt across my ass. "Or do you want to fuck you? It's your choice, butterfly."

I pondered his choices. As much as the belt excited me, the idea of his cock buried inside me appealed to me more. I wanted to orgasm.

"Make your choice fast or I'll decide for you, and you might not like what I choose."

"Fuck me," I breathed out. "I want you to fuck me."

He guided me up and leaned me against the sofa. When he inched closer to me, I tingled in anticipation of what was coming next.

"Oh!" I fell forward when he thrust inside me.

"Fuck!" He gripped my hips. "Always so wet and tight for me."

He pounded into me with determination and speed. If this man had a superpower, fucking would be it.

"I should take my belt to your pretty ass more often. "

"Yes." I felt no shame in letting him know I liked when he punished me. It seemed to work to my benefit. "Harder."

When he gave me what I wanted, his balls slapped against my ass. Each forward thrust got deeper and more brutal. I loved every second. I wanted to be the center of his world. The only woman he desired. The only one who could ever make him feel this way.

"Luciana..."

When he whispered my name, I couldn't hold on any longer. I clenched around his cock as he slowed his pace. I trembled, biting my bottom lip when he completely stopped moving, as if he could feel me unraveling. With him deep inside me, my climax rippled through me, fast and furious.

"I feel you, baby." He collapsed on my back, releasing his hot stream inside me. "All of you."

Our erratic breaths filled the room. I didn't know how long he stayed inside me, settling down, and controlling his breathing, but it would never be long enough. At that moment, he wasn't mad at me. We weren't fighting or hurting one another. I no longer had to betray him. We were finally right.

"That was amazing." He kissed my spine as he untied me, rubbing my wrists and then my arms and shoulders. Gently kissing my back and neck, before turning me to face him.

"You're not going to keep anything from me ever again, are you?"

"Lesson learned." I kissed him. "But there will be other punishments, right?"

"What am I going to do with you?"

"I can think of a few things."

CHAPTER 14

Romero

After I showered and got dressed, I came into the master bedroom to find Luciana still asleep in my bed. She was tired and still naked from yesterday's activities. After her spanking, I ordered dinner and had it delivered, so we never had to leave the bedroom. We hardly left the bed.

She was sleeping on her stomach, but the covers slipped off to reveal her back and the top of her sweet ass. The welts my belt had left would be a reminder to her today that she shouldn't lie to me again. I ran my hand down her spine, caressing her smooth skin. She stirred under my touch.

"Go back to sleep, baby." I leaned down and kissed her hair. "I couldn't resist touching you."

She rolled over. Her normally wide, expressive eyes were sleepy and confused. She sat up, pulling the sheet with her as she gazed around the room.

"You're in the master bedroom."

"You let me stay?"

Did she think I would just throw her out into the hallway after the night we shared? Yes, she probably did. Why?

Because I'm an asshole.

"I have to get up," she said.

"What's the rush?" I stroked her hair, trying to tame it from last night's sex. "You're not planning on another bikini-clad day by the pool, so all of my men can check you out, are you? Because I will shoot someone."

"I told you, that's a *you* problem. I can't help it if the men who work for you are pigs." She traced the pattern on the comforter. "I should be able to wear whatever I want and not worry about your men disrespecting me."

"You're absolutely right." I liked when she stood up to me. Well, within reason.

"I am?"

"That's why I would kill them and not you." I smirked. "What are your plans?"

"Stella is teaching me how to make gnocchi today."

"That's one of my favorites."

"I know." She smiled. "That's why she's teaching me."

"That's a very thoughtful thing for you to do."

"Don't thank me yet." She giggled. "You might not like the way I cook."

"The cookies you baked were delicious."

I would have given anything to crawl into bed with her and spend the day ravishing her, but Gio, Giancarlo, and Santino Marchelli were in my study waiting to discuss some of our latest problems.

"I'm working from home today." I took her hand and brushed her soft knuckles along my lips. "Do you want to have lunch with me?"

"Yes."

"Perfect." I gently kissed her. "Do you want to go out?"

"Like a date?"

"Sure." I ran my thumb across her lips and down her jaw. "I'll get us a table at the Marchelli winery. They have a fantastic lunch menu."

"That's where we met."

"I'm aware." The first time I saw her, we were at Santino and his wife Luca's wedding. "I couldn't take my eyes off you."

"You made me nervous."

"I still make you nervous." I kissed her again. "I'm going to be late."

"I'll see you later." She stretched before collapsing back into the pillows. "Have a good meeting."

She grabbed her phone and began scrolling,

looking like she belonged in that bed. Eventually, we'd have to revisit the sleeping arrangements.

As I walked down the hall, I realized I hadn't thought about her betrayal in hours. Not after we had sex, not after she fell asleep in my arms, and certainly not when we were together just now.

Am I forgiving her? Is that even possible?

When I joined the closed-door meeting in my study, the three were already discussing the reasons they thought the Torrios had this vendetta against my family.

They nodded as I took a seat at my desk, but continued their conversation.

"It doesn't make sense," Giancarlo said. "Antonio took over your father's territory long ago. You and Gio never challenged him. When he approached me about this alliance, I had no reason to believe he had an agenda."

"We were hasty." Gio leaned against my desk. "We saw an opportunity to move more merchandise through the ports and we thought the alliance with the Torrios would strengthen our position, but we should have researched more than we did."

That was Gio's polite way of saying, *I was too hasty because they dangled Luciana in front of me and I took the bait.* I didn't regret finding her, even if she came into this marriage with an agenda, but I should have taken more precautions. I took full responsibility for the situation we were in.

"The Torrios are a bigger threat than we anticipated," I said. "They got the Feds involved."

"Do you think Agent Morgan is dirty?" Giancarlo asked. "Is he working directly with Antonio?"

"No," Santino said. "My family believes the Torrios have an informant on the payroll, and they gave Morgan the information about the shipment."

"It's odd that they would send the agents after your legal shipment." Giancarlo raised his brow at me. "Why were they so sure it was an illegal product?"

"Who knows?" I didn't trust anyone but Gio to know how the Torrios came into possession of that knowledge. I had to protect my wife at all costs. "I have to figure out how to get out of this phony alliance."

"My brother Dominick told me to tell you whatever you need, just ask," Santino said. "You have the backing of the Marchelli family."

"We appreciate that." I watched the security cameras on my monitor as a black car pulled into the driveway.

"Do you want me to get that?" Gio pointed to the monitor.

"Salvi can handle it," I said. "What's this I hear about the two soldiers in the Lavanza family who were found dead in their car under the bridge this morning?"

"The council is looking into it." Giancarlo drank his coffee. "I'll let you know what they say."

"It's getting out of control," I shouted. "This is exactly why Gio and I didn't want to get involved with any of this. I should have stayed away from the families. We were doing fine internationally."

"The international climate was getting volatile with the cartels," Giancarlo reminded me. "You had to come back through the states and in order to do that, you needed the approval of the other families to move your product."

What he said made sense, but I didn't like it.

"Look how working with the Torrios worked out for me. They sold me out to the Feds. Now I have to lie low and I can't move my product."

"Be patient," Giancarlo told me.

"That's not his thing." Gio laughed. "He shoots first and asks questions later."

"Speaking of which," Santino said. "I backed the bureau off of the investigation into those four business associates of yours."

"How did you do that?" I asked.

"Someone owed me a favor, but there's no chance that will come back to you?"

"Not at all," I assured him.

"You do have to be patient," Giancarlo advised me. "Don't make the mistakes your father did."

"Patience? Do you really think the Torrios will get out of my way soon?" I pounded my fist on my desk. "Even with the backing of Santino's family, I can't remove Antonio from power. I don't want that war. His son's will avenge him."

Antonio and his three sons wouldn't go quietly, and they had the majority of the council on their side. Plus, as much as I hated to think about this, they were Luciana's family. It wouldn't be an easy fight.

"I want them to leave me alone," I said. "I want to know where this vendetta is coming from. Why did they pick a fight with me?"

"I'm sorry, but I don't have those answers." Giancarlo set his coffee cup on the end table. "We should have found out who was responsible for your father's death long ago, and maybe none of this would be happening."

"That's in the past," Gio said.

"You should have avenged his death." Giancarlo pointed at me. "I was in a position of strength then. We could have taken his territory together."

"I wasn't ready for that." I shook my head, but I knew he was right. The time for action was then. I had no claim to my father's territory now. I didn't even want it. I didn't need it. What I needed was a hassle free way to move my shit through the docks, but as long as the Torrios were in charge, I didn't see how that was going to be possible. I had to send a message. "Thank you both for stopping by this morning."

"Let me know what you need," Santino said.

"I'll be in touch." I nodded to Gio. "Can you see them out?"

Gio stood and opened the door for Santino and Giancarlo. I got up and poured myself a vodka. What a fucking mess! I had a shipment waiting on a boat in Mexico that I had to leave there because the Feds were watching me. None of the families were going to let me move anything now.

"Fuck!" I threw the glass against the wall. "Is that what you wanted, Antonio?"

"Feel better?" Gio stood in the doorway.

"Do you know how much money we lose every day that shipment sits there?"

"I do."

"I'm frustrated." I sat down.

"That wasn't a very productive meeting." Gio came back into the study "Giancarlo is getting too old for this business. So is Antonio, if he thinks he can come at us."

"He's already coming for us and has three powerful sons who will help him."

"Your plan worked. The Torrios took the bait and gave the shipment location to the Feds. Now we know for sure that they're after us."

"I can't send Luciana back there with more false information." I rubbed my temples. "They will figure it out. That was a one-shot deal." I came up with that idea when I was furious with her. I was either going to kill her or let her work off her betrayal. Now I didn't want any harm to come her way.

"We have to lie low. Our clients will understand." Gio sat on the edge of my desk. "No one wants to get caught."

"Giancarlo was right about the cartels," I said. "The international situation is too rough right now. We have to make a go of it here."

"We have the Marchellis." Gio looked at the security monitors. "We have to get the others on our side."

"That's easier said than done." I checked the monitor to see what had him so intrigued. "We need to figure out what Antonio wants with us."

"Speaking of which." He pointed to the screen. "Why do you think Kristina is here?"

"It can't be for any good reason, and if she's here to target my wife, it's not going to be Kristina Torrios' lucky day."

I am not in the mood...

CHAPTER 15

Luciana

I glided down the main staircase as Salvi answered the front door. I didn't even have a chance to come off my high of sleeping in Romero's arms last night when I heard the shrill voice of my aunt.

"I'm here to see my niece," her words echoed through the foyer. "Tell her I'm waiting."

"Mr. Bilotti doesn't like unannounced guests," Salvi informed her.

"I'm not here to see Mr. Bilotti," she said. "I'm here to see Luciana."

I had half a mind to sneak back upstairs and let Romero handle this, but I'd have to face her sooner or later.

"It's okay." I approached the door. "I'll see my aunt."

Salvi opened the door, and Aunt Kristina

strutted in. I'd rather take a meeting with a snake. It would be much more pleasant.

"You can excuse us," my aunt ordered Salvi.

Romero's guard looked at me for approval.

"It's fine." I nodded. "You can leave us. Thank you, Salvi."

"I'll be down the hall if you need me." He didn't acknowledge Kristina as he left the two of us in the foyer.

I waited for him to leave before speaking. "What brings you here?"

"I wish I could say it was a social call."

"Under what circumstances would you ever come to call on me socially?"

"You're right." She glanced around the foyer. "I'll get to the point."

"Please." I gritted my teeth.

"You came to see Vincent the other day," she said. "We thought you had useful information."

"I gave what I had to Vincent."

"Your information was useless," she said. "It was worth nothing, and we used huge favors because we thought you provided us with accurate details."

"How was I supposed to know what it was?" I stared down the hallway. It was only a matter of time before Romero joined this conversation. "You told me to get whatever I could. It's not my job to decipher what it is. That's supposed to be done on your end."

"Your job is whatever I say it is." She pointed in my face. "If you did a better job of screening the information before you brought it to us, we'd be in a better position by now."

"Do you know how secretive Romero is? How hard it was for me to even get that file?" *Okay, so Romero gave it to me, but the witch didn't need to know that.* "I can't take the time to research what I'm giving you."

"Excuses," she yelled. "Whose side are you on?"

"Why would you ask that question?"

"You gave us a location for a legal shipment," she said. "We wasted resources and the trust of a very well-placed informant. Do you know what that does to the Torrio credit on the street?"

That's what Romero wanted.

"Again, there was no way for me to know that." I hated being a double spy more than I hated being a regular spy. "I told you I didn't want this job."

"Your job is to spy for my family." She raised her voice, and if Romero hadn't already figured out our plan, he would have today. "Not to be the dutiful little bride of an arms dealer. Do you understand who owns you? It's not your husband, and if you forget that, you're in trouble."

"Lower your voice." I glanced over her shoulder, playing the part. "Romero and Gio are in the study."

"I told you if you did anything to get my family hurt or killed, I would kill you."

"What do you want from me?" I loathed this woman. "I have done everything you asked. Not just by marrying a man I didn't want to, but my whole life I've done whatever you people asked of me. Why? Because, in my warped reality, I wanted to belong to your twisted family. I wanted acceptance and God knows why, but love."

"Like that was ever going to happen."

"Don't worry, I'm not seeking any of that now." Love and acceptance were never going to happen for me. Not while I was in this dark and dangerous world.

"You finally wised up." She laughed. "Too little, too late, but you are under our control. You always will be. Once your husband figures out what you've done, that brutal man will kill you. I'm banking on it."

It's a good thing you're not a betting woman because I'm still alive.

"You're hardly the mastermind behind this operation." I wanted to wipe that satisfied smile right off her face. I wanted to tell her their plan had already failed because Romero had turned the tables on them. He outsmarted them and they had no idea.

"You believe what you want," she said. "If you screw up again, I will make sure they don't find your body. I'll do whatever I have to do to protect my family."

"Maybe if you were a better mother, none of your children would be in this situation."

She responded with a hard slap of her palm against my cheek. The assault was worth the satisfaction I got from seeing how much my words rattled her.

"You're going to regret that, you stupid bitch." The rage in my husband's voice should have terrified me, but it brought a strange sense of comfort in this moment.

Romero and Gio stood in the foyer. When did they get here?

"How dare you speak to me that way?" Kristina turned on her heel. "This is between me and Luciana. She knows her place."

"Too bad you don't." Romero came to stand by my side. "Who are you to come into my home and lay a hand on my wife? Do you think that will go unanswered?"

"What are you going to do?" Kristina placed her hand on her hip. "Hit me? Are you really your father's son, after all?"

That was a low blow.

"Mrs. Torrio," Gio intervened. "You should leave."

"Not until she hears my message loud and clear," Romero said. "You tell your husband if he wants to come at me, he comes himself. He doesn't send you to torment my wife."

"I don't know how you did it." My aunt looked at me. "But somehow you managed to do what I never thought you could."

If I didn't know better, I would think she was trying to tell Romero I had betrayed him. Why would she want him to know? Did she really want him to kill me?

"You're not listening to me," Romero shouted. "You go home and tell your husband if he has a problem with me, I want to hear it from him." When he stepped toward her, she backed away. "Do you understand me, Mrs. Torrio?"

"I'm not your messenger." She pushed him aside and moved toward the door, but he stood in her way, blocking her exit with his massive form. "Let me out of here."

"Remember the look in my eyes the next time you come back here because I will make you regret ever hurting my wife and I'm not just talking about hitting her. I'll make you suffer for everything you've done to her since the day she came to live in your wretched house." He moved out of the way and opened the door. "You're not welcome here anymore."

After everything I had done to him, he defended me.

"Such loyalty." My aunt smiled at me. "What do you think will happen when he turns on you?"

"Get out," Romero said. "Before it's too late."

My aunt hurried out the door, narrowly making it onto the porch before Romero slammed the door.

"I think you just started a war," Gio said.

"She hit you." Romero brushed his finger along my stinging flesh, ignoring his brother's observation.

"I'm okay," I said.

"Why didn't you fucking hit her back?" He growled as he took my hand and led me down the hall to the kitchen. "Well?"

"Why didn't I hit her back?"

"Yes." He lifted me onto the counter and went to the freezer for some ice. "She put her hands on you. That's unacceptable."

"It's not the way I react to things." I shrugged as he placed the ice in a plastic bag and wrapped it in a paper towel. "No one has ever hit me before. I didn't know what to do."

"You should have slapped that bitch."

When he pressed the ice to my cheek, I pulled back.

"Stay still," he ordered.

"It's cold."

"Next time, don't get hit."

"Are you mad?"

"I'm furious." He clenched his jaw tight. "But not at you."

"Oh." I let out a breath, trying to push back the panic attack I so desperately needed to have. "She's an unpleasant person. I don't know why I let her get to me."

"Because you have a dreadful history, and she doesn't want to see you happy."

Is that what I am? I didn't want to think about any of this now. Lies, secrets, and deception had become my entire existence. How much longer could I keep any of this up without breaking?

"Are we still going to lunch?"

"That's what you're worried about?"

"Well, I was looking forward to spending time with you."

"We're still going to lunch." He held the ice pack to my cheek. "What did she want?"

"To tell me how disappointed she was that the information I gave Vincent wasn't useful." I arched a brow at him. "You knew that already. That's why the raid was a bust yesterday."

"I needed to see what they would do with the information." He removed the ice and kissed my cheek. "I'm sorry she came at you."

"The way she came in here yelling, it was as if she wanted you to figure out what I am doing." Was my family ready to end this alliance? "She didn't care if you heard."

"She wants me to mistrust you." He pounded his fist on the counter. "She wants me to hurt you."

"You won't." I took his hand in mine. "You already know the truth and you didn't hurt me."

"That's debatable."

"You could have killed me." I bit my lip. "You wanted to."

"In that moment, yes, I did."

"I'm glad you didn't." I gazed into his eyes, wanting more than anything to take back everything I had done to him. "This is fine." I swiped my cheek. "Thanks for the ice."

"You should have clocked her." He shook his head. "I almost did."

"That would have gone over really well." My family's plan seemed to be unraveling before them. They underestimated Romero, but I had a feeling he wasn't done with them.

"Luciana, when I saw her hit you, I snapped." He squeezed my hand. "If Gio didn't hold me back, I would have come after her. There's something about her that's evil. The way she treats you is awful. I can't imagine what your life was like in that house."

"I try not to think about it."

"You have to defend yourself," he said. "I have to know that if anything happens to me, you can take care of yourself."

"What's going to happen to you?" Was Gio right? Was a war brewing?

"There's always a possibility something could happen to me, especially in my line of work." He cupped the side of my face in his hand. "Gio will look after you, but I'd feel better knowing your aunt isn't going to harass you for the rest of your life."

"I don't like this conversation." My heart rate increased with each breath I drew.

"It's reality." He pressed his lips to my forehead. "None of us are promised tomorrow."

"You can't leave me." My eyes filled with tears. "You're all I have."

"Luciana, I..."

"It's okay." I pressed my fingers to his lips because he didn't know what to do with my admission. "You should get back to work." I slipped off the counter. "I'm going to find Stella." I kissed his cheek. "I'll see you for lunch."

As I tried to make my getaway, he grabbed my hand and tugged me back to him.

"What?" I asked.

He took my face between his hands and brought my lips to his, answering my inquiry with a long, toe-curling kiss. When he pulled back, he wiped the tear that had escaped from my eye away with a gentle caress.

"For the record, I don't plan on going anywhere." He winked and then released me. "See you for lunch."

As he walked away, I wondered how much longer we could keep this up. I wondered the same thing when I was spying on him. He knew the truth, but I was in no better a position than I was when he didn't know. Now, I was betraying my family.

None of this turned out the way I thought it would. When I was forced into this relationship, I never imagined falling in love with Romero. But here I was. Alone, afraid, and in way too deep with a man who could end up being killed by my family or killing the only family I'd ever known.

I'm caught in the middle with no way out. Isn't that the story of my life?

CHAPTER 16

Romero

It was a few days after Kristina made her unwelcome appearance, and I hadn't heard a peep out of my in-laws. They moved their products freely in and out of the city, but I was still in a holding pattern. I couldn't trust the Feds wouldn't bust me. After their disasterous raid last week, they were gunning for me. I couldn't give them any ammunition.

"We have a problem," Gio said as he came into my study.

"Don't we fucking always?" I looked up from my laptop. "What is it now?"

"The cartel won't move anything internationally for us."

"Why not?"

"They think we're a liability." Gio ran his hand through his hair. "We were late on those two shipments. The Feds are sniffing around us. No one wants any attention."

"We were late because I used the sellers Antonio suggested and they sold me shit." I pushed a stack of papers off my desk. "I rectified it as quickly as I could. It didn't affect anyone's bottom line but ours. I made up for the missed deadline."

"I know, but because of the information Lu leaked to her family, the Torrios were able to get to the cartel. That's what they were doing in Florida last week. Word is that you dropped your guard. They know someone infiltrated your organization."

"The Torrios used the information to undermine me with the cartel." *Fucking wonderful.*

"It looks that way."

"I need the other families on my side." I rested my head against the back of my chair. "We need to make a bold move. I've let these people fuck me around long enough."

"What did you have in mind?"

"Find out when their next shipment is." I glanced at the doorway to find Luciana standing there. "Get back to me as soon as you know. I want to move as fast as possible."

Gio nodded before turning and greeting her. "Hey, Lu, how's it going?"

"Good." When she smiled, I wanted to forget everything that was going on in my world and focus only on her. "Can I come in?"

"Of course." I stood and came around my desk as Gio disappeared into the hall. I hoped he could get me what I needed today. I wasn't waiting any longer. It was time to take charge and fix my mistakes.

"I hope I didn't interrupt."

"Not at all." I held out my hand for hers. "What's up?"

"So, I was wondering, well, if you're not busy tonight." She rocked from side to side. "I mean, I know you're always busy, but I thought maybe..."

"Luciana, are you trying to ask me something?"

She nodded.

"Take a breath." I kissed her knuckles. "And start over."

"Okay." She inhaled and slowly let it out. "You know how I've been learning to make gnocchi?"

"Yes, Stella says you're doing a wonderful job." I smiled. "Despite all the pasta I've seen in the trashcan this week."

"Well, I wanted it to be perfect."

"I'm sure it is."

I liked seeing her have an interest in something other than worry. I also noticed while she was in the kitchen, she enjoyed the time she spent with Stella. With Stella's girls away at school and Luciana never having a maternal figure in her life, I had hoped this pairing would work out for both of them.

"I wanted to know if you would join me for

dinner tonight. I want to make dinner for you." She inched closer to me. "If you're going to be home."

"I'd love to have dinner with you." I wrapped my arms around her waist. "I've had a stressful few days, and dinner with you is exactly what I need."

"Really?"

"Yeah, butterfly, I think so." No woman I had dated had ever offered to make dinner for me. I appreciated the gesture.

"I don't know what's going on, but I'm sorry if anything I did before is causing you problems now."

This whole alliance really fucked things up for me. Her spying on me and reporting back to her family didn't help matters. At the end of the day, this was my fault. I should have been more aware of the situation I was getting myself into, but then I wouldn't have married her.

"Nothing is your fault." I kissed her neck, breathing in her light, summery scent. "I own my choices as much as I own my mistakes. I made this life and I don't regret much."

"You have to regret the Torrios." She rested her head on my chest. "We've caused so much trouble for you."

"*They* caused so much trouble for me."

"You and Gio were doing fine before the alliance. You didn't need them." She paused for a moment. "You didn't need me."

"How do you know what I needed?" I stroked her

hair. "I thought it was a mutually beneficial agreement. Giancarlo, my trusted advisor, thought so too. I agreed to it and I married you. I didn't have to. I chose to."

"Do you regret it?"

I wasn't ready to answer these questions. I saw the need in her eyes to hear what I had to say. Hear what she wanted me to say, but there was too much going on right now.

"Sorry to interrupt." Gio came back into the office.

Perfect timing, little brother.

"I have some information you'll want to hear," he said.

"I'll leave you to it." She stepped out of my hold. "I'll see you for dinner."

"I'll be here." I kissed her softly. "I'm looking forward to it."

She smiled at me before turning and leaving the room. Gio closed the door behind her.

"Looks like the two of you are finding your way back to one another," he said.

"Gio, I don't have time for this discussion."

"No, for real." He took a seat on the sofa across from my desk as I sat back down. "I'm curious what will happen if we go to war with her family?"

"What do you mean?"

"Well, right now, she's caught between two families. She's going to have to choose."

"She has to do what she has to do." I studied my computer screen, not really focused on what was on it. "It isn't an ideal situation for any of us."

"I believe she would choose you."

"Have I given her any reason to choose me?" I pushed back in my chair. "I married her against her will, I've been keeping her here as my prisoner, and I'm going to war with her family. Would you choose me?"

"That's not all your fault."

"But what choices has she had since we got married?"

"You've had a rough start, but you can salvage this." He stretched out his legs. "If you thought it was worth salvaging."

"This whole situation is fucked up." I slammed my fist on my desk. "I can't concentrate on my relationship with Luciana."

As much as I wanted to see where we could take things, we had some issues that needed to be resolved. None of them could be fixed until I dealt with the mess in my business.

"You said you had something I needed to hear."

"There's a last-minute shipment coming through the docks tonight," Gio said. "It arrives at the warehouse on Filter street."

"A Torrio warehouse." Interesting. Could this be the opportunity I had been waiting for?

"Our guy says it's been pretty hush, but he was able to get the details."

"What are they moving?" I had a gut feeling I wasn't going to like the answer.

"What the cartel says you can't."

"Fuck!" I stood from my desk. "That son-of-a-bitch wants my merchandise. Dad's territory is no longer enough for Antonio. He wants what we built."

"He wants to cut us out and take over the market for himself."

"That's why he needed this alliance." I sat on the edge of my desk. "He needed Luciana in here to get information on my shipments. He needed my contacts. My day-to-day operations. He could have all the outside spies he wanted but with her inside, she saw everything first hand."

"Even if she didn't know what she was seeing."

"We know from her texts and phone records she gave them enough to figure out how to get as far as they've gotten now." I closed my eyes, trying to come up with a way to retaliate. "They don't need her help anymore. That's why Kristina didn't care if I figured out what they were doing."

"They undermined your trust in the cartel. They put the Feds on us to create doubt."

"They made the cartel think I'm not a safe way to move anything. They shut down our operations in a matter of days."

"We underestimated them."

"No, Gio." I balled my fist and held it up. "They underestimated *us*."

"What do you want to do?"

"I want to blow it all up."

"I get that. We'll make them suffer," Gio said. "We just need a plan."

"No, you don't understand." For the first time in weeks, I was in control. "I want to literally blow up the whole fucking warehouse. We're going to destroy the shipment, and we're going to show them who's in charge."

"It'll definitely get their attention."

"Set it in motion. Blow it all up."

"You're sure?"

"If I can't move my product, neither will he." I smirked. "How's that for an alliance?"

CHAPTER 17

Luciana

I tossed another dress on the bed. Why couldn't I find the perfect one for tonight? I wanted this evening to be special. I needed a chance to show Romero how much I wanted our marriage. How much I wanted him.

As I pushed the hangers across the bar, I tried to find the best choice, but I kept passing the engagement dress. The red one that started it all. How I had despised that dress the night of our party. I hated it almost as much as I hated Romero. I took it out of the closet and held it up against my body, gazing in the mirror. Was the reason I couldn't find the most amazing dress to wear because I already knew in my heart that I should wear this one?

Our engagement party wasn't that long ago, but it seemed like an eternity. I continued to stare at myself in the mirror as I lost myself in the memory of that night.

"You've insulted me twice tonight, Luciana." I backed away when he came close, but he tugged me to him. He was rough and crude. Being this close to him gave me a strange feeling. One I wasn't familiar with.

"First, you were late, and then you refused my gift. Is that anyway to start our engagement?"

"I'm sorry." Why was I apologizing? Because he was scaring me and I didn't want to see his temper. "I didn't mean to offend you."

Why is he staring at my lips? Does he want to kiss me? *I hope he didn't try because I wasn't ready for that. I wasn't ready for him.*

"You can call me Lu." I tried to bring his attention back to the conversation.

"What?"

"You keep calling me Luciana but no one does."

"Isn't that your name?"

"Everyone calls me Lu." He needed to know these things about me if we were expected to get married.

"The sooner you realize I'm not like everyone else, Luciana, the better off you'll be."

"Why did you agree to this?" He didn't seem like the type of man who needed an arranged marriage. "Why do you want to marry me?"

"Because it benefits me and I always do what benefits me."

"So, it's just business for you?"

I didn't care one way or the other, but it would be nice to know what he thought about this silly arrangement.

"What is this about for you?"

Did he really want me to answer that?

"I know why I agreed," he said. "But why would you?"

"I, um, I didn't have a choice." What else could I say? Anything else would have been a lie and he would have seen right through it. "We should probably go inside now," I said. "They're waiting for us."

"We'll go inside after you change."

"Change what?" I didn't understand what he meant. My attitude? My composure? What did he expect me to change?

"Did you get it?" His brother joined us with something in his hand.

"Here." Gio handed Romero the red dress. The one I didn't want to wear. The one I left in my bedroom. "You must be Luciana."

I nodded, keeping my focus on the dress. He couldn't possibly expect me to change now? My eyes filled with tears when I realized that was exactly what he wanted me to do. I wiped the tears away because I wouldn't give him the satisfaction of letting him know he rattled me.

"This is my brother Gio," he said. "We'll meet you in the house in a few minutes."

"Okay." I really wished his brother would stay. In the little research I'd done on the Bilotti brothers, Gio seemed

to be the one with a calmer demeanor. The more reasonable brother.

Romero opened the back passenger door of his SUV. "Get in."

"Why?"

"Because I said so." *He gripped my elbow and violently shoved me into the car. No-one had ever handled me this way.*" Put this on. Now."

He threw the dress at me before slamming the door, causing me to jump.

"I already told you I'm not wearing this." *I tossed the dress back at him. How dare he treat me this way?*

"Maybe you didn't understand when I said I wouldn't tolerate your disrespect." *He came toward me, but I had nowhere to run. He pushed me down and got on top of me, pinning me against the cool leather of the seat.*

"Get off me!" *I pushed against him, but he was too strong for me to free myself.* "Stop it!"

I thrashed beneath him, hoping he would come to his senses. I had never been so afraid in my life. Why did he act this way? Why did he think this was acceptable behavior?

He grasped the front of my dress and ripped it down the center, exposing my bra and panties. His gaze devoured my flesh. I shook under his intense scrutiny.

"Please." *My chest rose and fell at a rapid tempo.*

"Please what?" *I tensed when he ran his finger along my throat and down my chest, tracing it over my nipple. "You caused this situation. I'm just correcting it."*

"You're an asshole."

"Tell me something I don't know." He circled his finger around my other nipple. "Your family gave you to me, Luciana."

They might have been true, but there was a reason they were giving me to him.

"All of you." He moved his hand down my stomach and to the edge of my panties. My breath hitched in my throat when he slipped his finger inside them. How far would he take this?

"No." When I wiggled beneath him, his erection pressed against me. This was turning him on?

"So, when you ask me if this is just business, the answer is yes." He kissed my neck, grazing his stubble along my skin." But that doesn't mean I won't claim every glorious inch of you and there isn't anything you can do about it."

When he got off of me, a sense of relief washed over me. He wasn't going to take this any further now. He threw the dress at me. "Wear this or your underwear. I don't care, but now we're late and that reflects on me."

"That dress is spectacular." Stella appeared in the mirror's reflection, pulling me from the memory.

"Yeah." I turned to face her. "Romero bought it for our engagement party."

"How sweet."

"I didn't think so that night." I draped the dress

over the back of the chair by the window. "I wasn't going to wear it."

"What changed your mind?"

"Romero." I could laugh now about the lack of choice he gave me, but that night I was scared, nervous, and wanted him to leave me alone. "In only a way he could."

"That sounds about right." She glanced at the bed with the pile of dresses. "All of these are stunning."

"I can't decide." I shrugged. "I want everything to be perfect."

"He already has you, Lu. Everything is perfect." She sat on the bed. "If he can't see what's right in front of him, he has the issue."

"He has his reasons."

"I'm with you every day. I see how lonely you are. There's no reason for that." She patted the spot next to her, so I took a seat. "Have you apologized for whatever you did to him?"

"Yes."

"But he won't forgive you?"

"I don't blame him." I smoothed my hand over the comforter. "He doesn't trust easily to begin with."

"I'm assuming your betrayal wasn't with another man because if it was, I don't think you'd still be in this house."

"I probably wouldn't be breathing." I laughed. "I didn't cheat on him. What I did was far worse."

"Maybe you need to forgive yourself for whatever it was." When she rubbed my back, I found her touch so comforting. "If you do that, then Romero can heal."

"I married him to get information for my family." The tears streamed down my face. "I didn't want to. They made me."

"That was an awful thing for them to ask of you." She put her arm around me. "They put you in a horrible position."

"I thought I could do it, but when I got to know Romero, I…"

"Fell in love with him."

I sobbed.

"It's okay." She hugged me.

"By the time I wanted to stop, it was too late. Romero figured it out, and now he can't forgive me." I rested my head on her shoulder because, for the first time since my mother was alive, someone understood what I needed. *A mom.* "I don't blame him. I hurt him."

"He's a difficult, complicated man." She let go of me. "He has so many demons. His father was a vicious, uncaring man. He treated Gio and Romero like possessions. He saw them as heirs to his empire. From the time they were young, he groomed them to be unforgiving. It's the only way Romero knows how to be."

"He can be caring and attentive." I nodded. "I've seen it."

"The fact that he didn't toss you out of here once he learned of your betrayal speaks volumes." She took my hand. "He brought me here so you would have someone to talk to. Someone to care for you."

"Like a mother."

"I know I can't replace yours, but Romero thought my presence here would be good for you." She smiled. "He is trying, Luciana. Give him a chance to forgive you."

"Thank you for listening and caring."

"Romero might have asked me to do it when he hired me, but the moment I met you, I knew it would be a simple task." She stood from the bed. "I'm going to finish up in the kitchen. I prepared the dining room for dinner and I put some champagne on ice."

"Thank you." I wiped my eyes. "I have a good feeling about tonight."

"I think you should wear the engagement dress." She pointed to the chair where I'd left the dress. "Romero will appreciate the gesture."

"I think you're right."

"Lu." She headed toward the door. "I hope after tonight you're back in the master bedroom."

"Me too."

Romero was late. He didn't like to be late, but here I was, sitting all alone and waiting for him.

I poured myself another glass of champagne. My second. The dinner I made had gone cold a while ago. No big deal. I could reheat it when he got home. I wanted to text him, but I didn't want to be a nag. He was only an hour late. He probably got caught up with his business. I didn't want to bother him because he was under a lot of stress.

I sipped my drink as I gazed out of the window overlooking the pool. If he let me put a tracker on his phone, I wouldn't be so anxious. At least I would know if he was on his way home. I could put the food back in the oven so it would be hot when he came through the door. I could pretend to be a traditional wife. *Who am I kidding?* Romero and I were far from traditional. Maybe I should text him and tell him I wanted dinner to be perfect, and I was wondering when he would be home.

I took another long sip of my sparkling drink. After a few minutes of staring at the clock, I picked up my phone and started a text.

Hey...

I stared at the screen for a few seconds before continuing.

Dinner is ready when you are.

Did that even sound right? Of course, dinner was ready, but he wasn't here. I deleted what I had and tried again.

Are you coming home for dinner? I cooked, remember?

Too aggressive? I didn't want him to think I was mad, even though I was slightly annoyed. I could just compose a text similar to what he would send me.

Where the fuck are you?

If I sent that one, he would probably storm home and take his frustrations out on me. Hmm... that wouldn't be a bad way for the evening to end. I backspaced my screen until there was no text.

I sat back down at the table, staring at my phone as if a text from Romero was going to magically pop up. If I had the tracker... *wait a second.* That social media page where those women were obsessed with the mafia, mainly Romero. If he was in the city, they would know.

Did I want to know?

I typed the name of the page into the search bar and started scrolling. I didn't have to scroll far because the first three posts were of Romero and Gio posing with several incredibly hot women, including Aria, the sexy club manager. I studied the picture of Aria and my husband. She was entirely too close to him. He appeared as if he was whispering into her ear. *What the hell?*

The timestamp on the post was ninety minutes ago. I had been waiting here like an idiot while he was out at his precious little club, taking pictures like some celebrity with every girl who was willing to drop her panties for him, including the one who ran his club and made him a ton of money every night.

I downed the rest of my drink, gathered up the plates, and marched down the hall to the guards' quarters. If my husband didn't want to eat dinner with me, I would find someone who would.

CHAPTER 18

Romero

The club was bursting at the seams tonight. The numbers were off the charts and the wait to get in grew each night. Since I took over, this place was the club to be. Celebrities, athletes, and society's elite frequented here on any given night. We had supermodels, movie producers, actors, and a senator or two. You name it and they were here. It didn't matter that an arms dealer owned the joint. They wanted in and I was more than happy to take their money.

Power was in the palm of my hand. No one was getting in my way. Not some FBI agent with a hard-one for my wife, and definitely not the Torrios. After tonight, they would feel my wrath.

"Are you happy?" Aria asked as she joined me at my back table. "The profits have been off the charts this week. We've never taken in this much money."

"You're doing a fantastic job." I didn't enjoy complimenting her, but I couldn't deny her skills when it came to managing my club. "I'm impressed."

"I'd like to take the credit, but people are showing up because you're here."

I downed my shot of vodka, pleased with the new product. Despite the delay at the docks, the shipment made it to the club.

"You don't believe me?" She sat across from me. "It's all over social media."

"Is it?" I tried not to pay attention to any of that.

"When someone spots you in here, they make a post and it gets shared. The next thing you know, we are at capacity."

"You wouldn't happen to be doing some of the sharing, would you?"

"It's good business sense. If we create a buzz, people want to see you and Gio."

"I'm here checking on my investment." I looked over at the crowded dance floor. "If that brings them here, then it's a bonus."

"You've been here a lot this week. The sales at the door are at an all-time high."

"We switched distributors, we've hired new staff, and we're remodeling the upstairs bar. It's been a busy week. I thought it best for me to make a few appearances." I leaned back in my chair. "People need to know I'm in charge."

"I noticed you don't bring your wife." She traced

her finger along the table, inching closer to my hand. "Why is that?"

"That's none of your business."

I hadn't brought Luciana back here because I couldn't run the risk of that annoying FBI agent being here. If I saw him show concern for my wife one more time, I would kill him. I didn't need that kind of aggravation. It was safer for me to leave her home.

"It's just that in my experience, men like you like to flaunt their wives."

"Men like me?" I tapped my fingers on the smooth granite table. "What do you think you know about a man like me?"

"Plenty."

"Another round for everyone." I pointed to my shot glass when the server came to my table. "Why don't you enlighten me," I said to Aria, who was quickly getting on my last nerve. If she wasn't so good at her job, I'd toss her out on her Brazilian butt-lifted ass, butte was good for business. For now, she would stay, but I had a feeling her days were numbered.

"Rich. powerful, domineering."

"I won't deny I'm all of those things." She wasn't making any ground-breaking observations.

"Men like you usually have their wife or girlfriend with them at all times." She shrugged. "If they don't, well, I have to wonder why."

"Luciana doesn't need to come to the club with me every time I'm here."

"She trusts you?"

"She has every reason to trust me." I studied the steady stream of customers filing through the door. "Shouldn't you be working?"

No matter how good she was, no one was irreplaceable. Her flirtatious personality would have been intriguing if I had found her the least bit attractive. There was something about her I didn't like. I also didn't want to be with anyone but my wife.

The server brought the next round of shots as Gio arrived with three women I'd never seen before.

"Looks like we're just in time." He grabbed a shot glass off the server's tray. "I met these three beautiful women, and they wanted to take a picture with us."

"No." I glared at him. "It'll end up all over social media."

So many of these women were obsessed with snapping a picture with a gangster. Before Luciana, if I wanted to spend the night with a woman, she had to agree to leave her phone with Salvi. I didn't need my junk ending up on social media. Some of these women were so obsessed, they spent their time creating pages and accounts dedicated to me, Gio, Rocco, Vincent, Sandro, and all the Marchelli brothers. It was insane.

"That's exactly what we need." My brother downed his shot. "Public exposure."

An alibi. That was what we were all doing here.

"Please." The redhead with the big boobs and the green eyes smiled at me. "Just one picture."

"Maybe a drink," her friend with the platinum blonde hair and fake lips said.

If these women had half the grace and beauty my butterfly had, they wouldn't have to beg for pictures and drinks with men like me. They would have their own men who could take care of them.

One of the reasons I had been drawn to Luciana was because she was so different from the women who wanted my attention. She wanted to know me. Not for my money, and not for my last name. If her family hadn't fucked up our marriage, we would be in a better place now.

"Fine." I waved Salvi over. "Take some pictures for us."

Aria slipped off her chair and came to stand between me and Gio. "Two Biiottis" She tossed her hair to the side and leaned into me. "Wouldn't that be something?"

"In your dreams," I whispered into her ear as Salvi took the picture.

"Hey, Aria." Gio winked at her. "My brother is taken, but I'm single."

"I'll keep that in mind." She shimmied past him, rubbing against him as she devoured me with her gaze. "I need to get back to work."

"Take these people with you." I circled my hand

in the air. "Drinks are on me. Set them up in one of the VIP lounges."

"You heard my brother," Gio yelled over the music. "Anyone who doesn't work for us should clear out. Follow Aria. She'll hook you up with some free drinks."

The red head whispered something into Gio's ear and he nodded before kissing her cheek. The group who had been hanging around us for most of the night dispersed into a back room to enjoy the rest of their night on me.

"You'd fuck Aria?" I asked, half-disgusted at him.

"If there was no Luciana, you wouldn't?"

"Maybe a lifetime ago, but not now." I shook my head. "She's high maintenance and only seeks what I could do for her."

"I only need one night." He laughed. "I'd fuck her brains out, and she'd get us out of her system."

"She doesn't deserve you."

"Since when did I ever gauge whether the woman I was going to fuck deserved me?"

"Maybe that's your problem."

"Are you giving me advice on my love life?" He handed the server a hundred-dollar bill. "My glass shouldn't be empty."

"Yes, Mr. Bilotti." She lingered for a moment, staring at us.

"That means we need more drinks, sweetheart." I

smiled at her, mesmerizing her a little more. "Don't make us wait."

As she hurried off to fill our request, Gio couldn't keep his eyes off her ass. Aria, the redhead, and now the server. I didn't miss the single life.

"Back to the advice." He laughed. "I'm dying to hear what you have to say."

"Why is it so funny?"

"Ah, because your love life isn't exactly on point."

"How do you know?"

"How do I know?" He rolled his eyes. "Because I've been there every step of the way."

"Not every step." *You're not there when she screams my name and begs for more.* "We have our moments."

"I'll bet." His phone lit up with a text.

"What is it?"

"It's done." Gio picked up his shot glass and held it up.

"Good." I clinked my glass to his. "Now maybe we can get on with business."

"You struck back. Now they will know you're in a position of strength."

"Torrio might not realize it was us right away, but this setback should slow him down and we can figure out how to undo the damage he has done to our business."

"Tonight's a start." He set his glass down. "You want to go get dinner?"

"I am a little hungry. Oh shit."

"What's wrong?"

"Dinner? What time is it?"

"It's late for dinner, but we have to eat."

"Shit!" I looked at my watch. "We've been here for hours."

"Coordinating and organizing blowing up shit takes time."

"I was supposed to be home for dinner." How had I forgotten that? "Luciana is making me dinner."

"Oh, well, that sucks."

"Fuck, Gio." I took my phone out of my pocket, hoping I could fix this. "She hasn't called or texted."

"That's not a good sign. That means she's pissed."

I'd been so preoccupied with striking back at Antonio I had completely lost track of time. I called Luciana, but it went straight to voicemail. She wasn't even sitting by her phone waiting for me to call.

"I have to go." I got up from the table. "Can you settle up here?"

"Sure." He took out his credit card. "I'll be by the house soon. I want to make some calls and see what I can find out on the street."

He could have done that from the penthouse, but he wanted to come to the house in case things got out of control with me and Luciana. I didn't have time to argue with him. Maybe we would need a referee.

"Don't you have one or two or three women you could spend the night with?" I asked.

"They'll be here tomorrow night." He smirked." Or at least more like them. Now that you're off the market, my possibilities have increased."

"These are not the women you want." I looked around for Salvi. "Trust me. Find someone who wants you for you." Like the woman I had at home. The one who I had mistreated and hurt these last few weeks. "Find a woman who doesn't care about your money, status, or what you can give her."

"Lu's taken."

"Yeah, she is, even if she doesn't know it."

"Romero, here's a foreign concept, but when you get home," Gio said. "You should apologize."

He was right, but something told me apologizing wasn't going to be enough this time.

CHAPTER 19

Luciana

As I cleaned up the kitchen, Jag and Joey loaded the plates into the dishwasher. I finished the bottle of champagne and we opened a bottle of wine, but the guys didn't want to drink. Apparently, they were on duty and had to keep an eye on me, so they watched while I drank.

"Thanks for a fantastic meal, Lu," Jag said.

"It's the first time I ever cooked anything." I wiped the counter. "I'm glad you enjoyed it."

"It was delicious." Joey dried his hands with a paper towel. "I'm sorry the boss missed it. He probably got caught up with something."

"His loss." I tried to hide my disappointment, but having dinner with them kept my mind off Romero's lack of interest in the evening. I hadn't even looked at my phone in over an hour.

"Maybe you two can still have your night." Joey looked at his phone. "Romero is on his way in now."

"We should probably go back to the monitors," Jag said. "We've been in the kitchen for a while."

"You don't have to run away because he is home." I refilled my glass, hoping the wine would help suppress my anger.

The alarm panel chimed, alerting us that Romero had entered the house. His heavy footsteps pounded against the floor, causing my stomach to turn. As the sound grew louder, my heart rate increased. The anger and frustration that had built inside me over the last few hours bubbled to the surface and when he appeared in the doorway of the kitchen, it came to a head.

He stared at me for a moment and then glanced around the room, accessing the situation. He looked annoyed, but that was comical, considering I was the one who got screwed over tonight.

"Romero," Joey said. "You're home."

"Lu made us the most amazing dinner." Jag awkwardly motioned toward me. "It was superb."

"Get out." Romero pointed at the door without taking his gaze away from me.

Joey and Jag hurried from the kitchen without saying another word, leaving me with the monster who I had feared for so long.

"Don't be mad at them for keeping me company."

"They're supposed to be working, not eating dinner."

"Someone had to eat it."

I came around the island, trying to make my way to the back staircase, but he moved to block the steps.

"Luciana." He reached for my hand, but I backed away, knowing it would make him mad but I didn't care. "I'm sorry I'm late."

"Late?"

"I'm more than late, but it couldn't be helped." He removed his jacket and loosened his tie. "It was business."

"You didn't even call."

"The night got away from me." He sighed. "There was an important business deal that I had to take care of. I can't talk about it, but it's done now."

"Did your business deal require you to drink shots and spend the night with your slutty club manager?"

"Those fucking pictures." He slammed his fist against the wall. "That's not what I was doing."

"How can you deny it when I saw the pictures?" I shouted. "She was hanging all over you. It didn't look like you were conducting any business. It was all pleasure."

"You couldn't be more wrong." When he stepped closer to me, I backed away. "Stop doing that." He grabbed my arm and tugged me to him. "I needed to be in the public eye tonight. I can't tell you why, but there was a reason I was at the club."

"I don't care what you were doing there." I tried to struggle out of his grasp, but it only made him hold me tighter. "Let go of me."

"No." He took a breath. "When I realized how late it was, I called you. I texted you several times from the car on my way home, but you didn't respond."

"My phone is in the dining room." I was getting nowhere so I stopped struggling. "After a few hours, I got tired of waiting for you and I really didn't care if you called or not."

"I don't believe that you didn't care."

"Why? Because I'm such a fragile pushover?"

"No."

"Why do you insist on punishing me for what I did? Are you ever going to put that in the past?"

"That's not what tonight was about. I got caught up with work. I said I was sorry."

"Like I've said, I was sorry so many times before and you won't accept my apology?"

"I don't want to fight with you."

"You don't think I have a breaking point?"

"I'm sure you do, but tonight isn't it." He wrapped his arms around me and brought me close to him. "I said I was sorry for being late. I didn't mean to upset you. We can still salvage the evening." He swept his lips along my jaw. "I know you want to."

My knees buckled when he trailed his lips across my heated skin. The scent of alcohol lingered on his breath, reminding me he didn't spend the night with me.

"No." I pushed against his chest. "You're not going to solve this by seducing me."

"Are you sure?" He grabbed my backside, possessively squeezing it. "You don't have the luxury of saying no to me." He ran his tongue across my lips. "You don't want to say no to me. I can see it in your eyes. I can hear it in your voice."

The bastard was right. I didn't want to say no to him, but I had to. We needed to stop this game we had been playing since the second we met.

"I don't want to." When I shoved him, he released me.

He grinned, but I saw the shock in his eyes.

"You don't want to?" He laughed as if my words didn't matter.

"No." I stood my ground. "You can't just hurt me like you do and then expect me to forgive and forget."

"Are you kidding me?"

Maybe *forgive and forget* wasn't the right term, considering what I had done to him. I had traveled down the path of no return so I needed to keep going if I wanted to be heard.

"How much longer are you going to punish me for what my family made me do?"

"As long as I want to." He advanced me, pinning me against his intimidating form and the counter. "I fucked up tonight, but that is nothing compared to the betrayal you committed against me."

"I've apologized for that, but you won't hear it."

"I don't want to talk about that now." He gripped my chin in his firm grasp. "I want to finish the rest of this evening with you." When he pushed against me, his erection brushed my thigh. "I want you."

"No."

"That isn't how this works, butterfly." He dipped his head and licked his lips. "You know that."

"Romero." I tried to pull away, but he pressed his lips to mine, pushing his tongue inside my mouth and kissing me until I couldn't protest. I didn't want to fight with him, but I didn't want things to continue the way they had been. Only I had the power to change that.

"Stop." I turned my face, but that only fueled his fire.

"You know I like it when you fight me. It makes me fuck you that much harder." He slid his hand under my dress. "Did you wear this for me?"

"Does it matter?"

"You look amazing." He kissed my neck as he rubbed his fingers over my panties, touching me where I needed him most. *Strength! Where is my strength?* I had none when it came to him. I wanted him as much as he wanted me, and he knew it.

I squeezed my legs shut and swatted his hand away. "I don't want to have sex with you."

"I don't believe you." He hitched my leg over his hip and thrust his pelvis forward, making me feel what he wanted. "You're not going to stop me." He lowered his lips to my breasts as he gripped my hip. "Let me fuck you. We will both feel better after. I promise."

My body tensed when he reached for his belt buckle. Something inside me snapped. He wasn't taking me seriously. When he reached under my dress and tugged at my panties, I looked into his eyes, fighting the lust in his with everything I had.

"You'll have to force me," I said in a shaky voice. "I won't let you have me."

"What?"

"I'm not going to consent."

He let go of me and backed away.

"You think I would..." He ran his hand through his hair. "I've never forced myself on anyone."

"I wanted you to stop because we can't keep going like this. You weren't listening to me."

"We can't keep going like what?"

"We fight, we hurt one another, we have sex, and we repeat it all again the next day." I tugged on the hem of my dress, trying to put it back in place. "I'm exhausted."

"What do you want from me, Luciana?"

"You can start by telling me what was so important that you had to stay at the club all night."

"I had business."

"What kind of business?" I threw my hands in the air. "I thought the club was legitimate."

"It is."

"Then why can't you tell me what you were doing?" It wasn't even about what he was doing. I just wanted him to tell me.

"I don't answer to you."

"You don't trust me."

His silence told me everything I needed to know.

"You think I'm still working for my family?"

"You wouldn't do that to me again." He clenched his jaw. His tone was low and deadly. "I hope you won't do that to me again because I won't be as kind as I was last time."

"Do you trust me, Romero?"

"Don't ask me that now." He pounded his fist on the counter. "I can't answer that."

"Why?" I yelled. "When will you be able to answer it?"

"Trust isn't something I give away." His calm voice articulated his argument, but his eyes were cold. "It has to be earned. I have to know that when I place my trust and loyalty with someone, they will reciprocate it. If I bring in the wrong people, it could get me killed. It could get my brother killed. My men killed."

"Am I the wrong people?"

"Your family is." He paced the kitchen. "Now they're trying to take what's mine. They're trying to destroy everything I've built," he shouted. "I won't have it. I won't let them bring me down."

"When you look at me, do you see my family?" How could he not? If they didn't use me as a weapon, they couldn't have gotten to Romero.

"When I look at you, I'm reminded of what they did to me, what they made you do to me." He leaned against the wall. "I don't want to see any of that, but it's there and I don't know what to do with all this rage. We could have had a life if they held up their end of the bargain. None of you had any intention of making an alliance. You entered into this marriage with lies and deception. You did this, not me."

"You're never going to forgive me," I whispered. "You're not capable of it."

His emerald gaze burned into mine, but he remained silent. Maybe he was afraid of what he might say. Once the words were spoken, he couldn't take them back. Was he done hurting me? Making me pay for what I'd done? How much longer did he expect me to stay here and wait for him to let me in?

One of us had to end all this toxic tension. I was being honest when I said I was exhausted. Mentally, physically, I wasn't strong enough for this life. I certainly wasn't meant to handle his rejection one more day. I wasn't built for this.

"Romero." I reached for the rings on my left hand and slipped them over my knuckle. "I can't do this anymore."

"Luciana." He stepped toward me. "Don't you fucking dare."

"Why not?" Say something to make me change my mind. "Give me a reason to stay."

He dropped his gaze to my finger as I removed his mother's rings and placed them on the counter.

"I'm out." I turned and bolted for the hallway, knowing I had little a chance to get upstairs before he grabbed me, especially not in these heels.

"The fuck you are. You don't decide when this is over." His heavy footsteps were right behind me as I made my way to the staircase. "You don't get to walk away from me."

As I approached the steps, Gio stood in front of them. When our eyes connected, he nodded and moved out of my way. He once told me if I stood up to Romero, he would respect me. God, I hoped it was right.

"Gio." Romero shouted. "Get out of my way!"

I hurried upstairs and ran down the hall to the guest bedroom. I slammed and locked the door as fast as I could. The only reason I made it this far was because Gio made sure of it. They yelled at one another, but I didn't care what they were saying. I didn't have much time. Once I removed those rings from my finger, I released the beast within my husband. If he considered spying on him a betrayal, what I had just done was a hundred times worse than that.

Would I survive his wrath this time?

CHAPTER 20

*R*omero

"Gio, get out of my way!" I didn't have time for his therapy session. I needed to get to Luciana and settle our shit tonight. This had gone on way too long. That was my fault, but I never expected her to walk out on me.

My brother crossed his arms over his chest and blocked me from going after my wife.

"I can't deal with the both of you." I threw my hand in the air. "Aren't you supposed to be on my side?"

"I'm always on your side."

"You have a strange way of showing it."

"Leave her alone," he said. "You need to calm down before you can settle anything with Lu."

"I need you to get out of the middle of my marriage." The anger brewing from this situation was transferring from Luciana to Gio. At least I could hit him. It might make me feel better.

"Because you're doing such a spectacular job of being her husband?"

"Fuck you." I pushed him. "I have to go after her."

He pushed me back.

"Back off or you'll regret it," I said.

"I'd rather you go a few rounds with me than with her."

"How many times do I have to tell you I am not our father?"

"Here's some unsolicited advice." He pointed at me. "If you can't trust her, let her go. If she's only here for you to torture, let her go." He relaxed his stance and took a deep breath. "This isn't healthy for either of you and it's not fair to her."

"Fuck." I hated he was right. "I'm not going to say it again. Move."

"Fine." He stepped aside. "If you hurt her, I'll kill you."

"I won't hurt her." I ran up the steps. "I'm going to do what I should have done a long time ago."

"I hope it's the right thing."

"Don't think we're not going to address that you threatened me." I yelled over my shoulder. "Asshole."

"Back at you, asshole."

As I got to the bedroom door, I tried to calm

down, but I only became more enraged. When I opened my hand, the shiny diamonds gleamed in my palm. How dare she take these off and tell me it was over? She didn't get to say we were over. After everything she had done to me, she wanted to end it because I forgot about our dinner? It was more about dinner, but still. She wasn't leaving me.

I shoved the rings inside my pocket and then turned the handle on the door. I wasn't shocked it was locked, but it still pissed me off.

"Luciana, open the door," I pounded on it. "Now."

"Go away."

"Do you think a lock is going to keep me out?" I banged harder. "Let me in."

"No!"

"Let's keep this civilized." It took all my effort to give her the chance to open the door on her own, but my patience was wearing thin.

"I said go away."

"Damn it, Luciana." With one swift, hard hit of my foot, the door broke open and busted off the frame.

"What the hell are you doing?" She launched her stiletto at me, but her aim was pitifully off and it landed in the hallway. "Get out of here."

"I once told you, I didn't have the patience for your defiance." I advanced her, blocking her in the corner of the room. "This is definitely one of those times."

"You don't have the patience for me?" When she reached to push me out of the way, I grabbed her wrist. "I lost mine for you a long time ago."

"Really?" She tried to struggle, but she should have known by now that she wasn't getting away unless I let her. "If I recall, I'm not the one who blew this marriage apart before it even got started. I'm not the one who lied for weeks."

"Maybe if we could have discussed what I had done like human beings instead of you trying to choke me and hold me prisoner, things wouldn't have gotten this far."

"You're right." I let go of her hand and sat on the bed because I couldn't argue with her. The way I handled things was atrocious.

"I am?" She backed away from me.

"I could have handled the situation a lot different, but I didn't. And you didn't come to me when your family made you betray me, even when you knew I would help you."

"We were both wrong."

"I don't know what you want from me." That wasn't true. She wanted me to forgive her. I wanted to forgive her. I wanted to trust her and believe she would stand beside me no matter what. Was that too much to ask? Isn't that what married people did? Support one another?

"I want so many things." She hesitantly inched toward me, but stopped before she got too close. That annoyed me. She shouldn't be afraid to come near me.

When I stood, she pulled back further until she hit the wall.

"I hate when you do that."

"Maybe if you weren't so scary."

"There's nowhere for you to run." I closed the space between us. "I won't let you. We have to figure this out."

"I can't do this anymore."

"Tell me what you want." I cupped the side of her face in my hand, hating the way she trembled when I was close. "Tell me what you need."

"I need a husband who will protect and cherish me." A tear slid down her cheek. "I want a friend. Someone who cares about me the way I care about them."

I wiped the tear from her face, trying to be gentle. Her anguish and pain rattled me in ways I didn't expect.

"I want more than sex." She gazed down at the floor. "I need more. Even if I screwed up, I deserve a second chance."

"I don't give second chances."

"Then you have to let me go," she whispered. "Please."

"No." I brought her lips to mine and slowly

kissed her, savoring her taste, relishing in her soft touch.

She pushed against my chest in a weak attempt to stop me, but I didn't relent. I held her in my arms, kissing her until we were both breathless and calmer than a few minutes ago.

"Lu, I want to be the man you need." I let go of her. "I've always wanted to be him because I knew I wasn't worthy of you. You betrayed me and I lashed out at you. I kept telling myself it was because I don't forgive. That wasn't it at all."

She reached for my hand, throwing me off balance. She wasn't retreating. Wasn't trying to run away from me.

"I made you suffer for what you had done to me because..." I took her face between my hands. "Because I love you." My heart raced. "As fucked up as that sounds, it's the truth. You are the only one who has the power to rip my heart to shreds, and when you betrayed me, that's exactly what you did."

"Oh." She gasped.

"When I found out what you had done to me, I didn't know what to do or what to think. For the first time in my life, I couldn't trust my instincts."

"You called me Lu."

"After everything I admitted, that's what you took away from this?"

"No." She laughed. Really laughed. Like she was

happy. I made her fucking laugh. "I love you too, Romero. So much."

"I'm sorry for the way things turned out between us. They put you in a horrible position, and I reacted the same way your family would have. I treated you no better than they did. For that, I'm truly sorry."

"I'm sorry I didn't trust you enough to tell you what they were making me do. I was so scared, and I didn't know what to do."

"From now on, there can be no more secrets." I pressed my lips to hers. "We're stronger together."

"Have you…" She tensed. "I mean, can you…"

"Forgive you?" I reached into my pocket and took out her wedding rings. "Only if you'll put these back on and never take them off."

When she held out her shaky hand, relief poured over me.

"I never want to take them off again."

"When things settle down and I figure out how to deal with your family, I want to marry you all over again. I want to do it for real." I slipped the rings on her finger. "I want you to know it will be forever and I'll never let you doubt my trust again."

"A real wedding?" She shook her head. "Not that sham we called a wedding the first time?"

"I promise to love you, respect you, and always cherish you."

"I want to be your wife in every sense of the

word. I want to love, honor, and be loyal to you forever."

I wrapped my arms around her waist and kissed her slowly, taking my time to show her how much I wanted her. How much I needed her.

"I know you said we have to be more than sex, but right now, I want to make love to you. Like I never have before."

"I won't stop you." She reached for the buttons on my shirt and undid them as she kissed my neck. Once she pushed my shirt over my shoulders and it fell to the floor, she unbuckled my belt.

"Wait." I scooped her up in my arms and carried her to the door, hanging off the hinges.

"Where are we going?" She glanced over her shoulder. "There's a bed right over there."

"That's not *our* bed." I carried her down the hall and to the master bedroom. "From now on, the only place you'll ever sleep is with me."

Once we reached the bedroom, I shut the door with my foot and brought her to the bed. Setting her at the edge, I tangled my fingers in her hair and kissed her mouth, swirling my tongue around hers. As she undid my pants, I slipped off my shoes, and then reached down to take off my socks.

When my pants hit the floor, I stepped out of them and kicked them to the side. As we continued to kiss, she reached inside my boxer briefs and took my cock in her hand, sliding her silky palm up and down my shaft.

We smiled at one another between kisses, making the moment light and playful. Her relaxed demeanor caught me off guard. I was so used to her shying away from me, or her waiting for me to tell her what to do.

"Luciana." I moaned as she rubbed her thumb over my tip, spreading the pre-cum that seeped out along the head.

I reached for her zipper, slowly lowering it until it would go no further.

"You wore this for me, didn't you?" I trailed my fingers down her neck and to the thin strap on her shoulder. "I gave this to you the night you became mine."

"I was afraid to be yours then." She kissed my chest.

"How about now?" I pushed the other strap down, letting the dress fall to the floor. "Do you want to be mine now?"

"You know I do." She released me from her hold, stepped back, and shimmied out of her red lace panties. "I want you to be mine, too."

"You're the only one I'll ever belong to."

She laid back on the bed, cupping her breasts in her hands and squeezing them as she spread her legs open, revealing her bare, glistening pussy.

"Fuck," I whispered, knowing I had to control my

urges. I had to slow this down and show her how much she meant to me.

I yanked off my underwear and dropped to my knees, taking her ankles in my hands and resting her legs over my shoulders. Licking my lips, I pushed my fingers inside her, moving them in and out before lowering my face between her legs and feasting on her hot, wet folds.

She lifted her hips off the bed and thrust them into my face, forcing me to fuck her with my tongue. She continued to play with her tits, twisting her nipples and squeezing her mounds in her palms.

I shifted my waist forward, practically fucking the bed because my balls ached for release. I slid my hands under her ass, licking and sucking her until her legs quivered on either side of my neck.

"Romero..." Before she even finished her orgasm, I climbed on top of her, hitched her leg over my hip, and sunk my cock deep inside her. She panted as she gazed into my eyes, a soft smile playing at her lips.

"I love you," I whispered against her mouth. "More than I ever knew possible."

"I love you too." She ran her hands up and down my back. "I love us."

I moved inside her at an unhurried tempo, taking my time to feel her, to please her, to love her. It had never been this way for me before, but then again, it could only ever be this way with her. After a few moments, our bodies tensed and, as if we were one in complete sync, we released together. She quieted my restless soul and gave me everything I would ever need. Now I had to be the man she deserved. The one who would always protect, love, and cherish her. She was my entire world.

"I'm sorry." I took her face between my hands. "I never want to hurt you again."

"Don't apologize," she whispered. "We had to happen the way we did, so we could be who we are right now."

"Together."

"Always."

We spent the rest of the night making slow, passionate love. With every breath I took, I felt like she was breathing for me. I wouldn't go back to a life where Luciana didn't exist, but how long would it take for my sins to catch up to me?

CHAPTER 21

Luciana

The room was dark as a buzz hummed from some place distant in the room. I cuddled closer to Romero. For the first time in a long time, I was secure and wasn't afraid of what the new day would bring. I kept my eyes closed, trying to settle back to sleep, but the buzzing grew louder, more consistent.

"Fuck." Romero fumbled next to me, reaching out.

"What is it?" I didn't open my eyes.

"My phone, baby." He sat up and answered it. "What?"

I rolled onto my side and breathed into his pillow. It was warm and comforting.

"This morning?" Romero asked the person on the other end of the line. "I think that's our best option."

He paused for a moment, probably listening to what the caller had to say. It must have been important for them to call in the middle of the night, but this was hardly a nine-to-five business.

"Set it up," Romero said. "Have Santino come with us. We'll need him to undo all the legal bullshit and get us the hell out of this mess."

Was he talking about the mess my family had caused? The mess I helped to make?

"Yes, I know what today is. You don't have to remind me."

What's today? July twelfth, I think.

"Gio." Romero took a second to speak. "Thanks for last night."

He waited a few seconds for Gio to respond.

"Asshole." He laughed. "Yes, that's me apologizing. That's what she would have wanted."

She?

He ended the call, but stayed in a seated position for a few minutes. I sat up and draped my arms over his shoulders.

"Is everything okay?" I kissed the back of his neck, breathing in his cinnamon and spice scent that mingled with my perfume.

"It will be." He patted my hand. "Gio and I have to have an early meeting."

"With my uncle?"

He nodded.

"Are you sure that's a good idea?"

"I have to resolve whatever is going on between my organization and Antonio's. He has a serious vendetta against me, but I don't know why."

"I wish I knew why they came after you."

"It's not your job to know." He turned to face me. "This is all me."

"What do you plan to do with my family?" Romero had to do what he had to do to protect his territory and shipments, but my family would fight as hard as they could. "I know they started this."

"I need to finish it." He stroked my cheek. "You don't need to worry about anything. I'll protect us. I'll do whatever it takes to get out of this peacefully. There might be a battle. Things were set in motion last night, but I'll try to settle it without casualties."

"You can't promise that." I wasn't asking him to make any promises, but I couldn't bear the thought of anyone dying, especially not my husband.

"No, I can't, but I'll try to negotiate a solution that works for both families. I never wanted a war." He switched on the lamp, and then opened the drawer by the bed and took out a pale blue square box. "I don't want you to worry about any of this. Now, you are out of this. You don't have to spy on anyone. You don't have to bring back information or do anything that will put you in danger. I will take care of you."

"I would still do whatever you needed."

"I appreciate that." He kissed my cheek. "I don't need you to do anything but love me."

"That's the easy part." I glanced at the box. "What's that?"

"I got this for you a while ago." He handed it to me. "I planned to give it to you the night we were going to go to the movie theater, but then shit happened."

"Like you found out what I'd been doing for my family." Romero may have forgiven me, but I wasn't sure I'd ever be able to forgive myself for hurting him.

"I don't want to think about that anymore." He ran his hand along my back. "It's in the past and we're going to leave it there."

"Okay." I lifted the lid on the box to reveal a stunning diamond bangle bracelet. "Romero." I gazed up at him, taken in by the gesture of his gift. "This is gorgeous."

"Do you like it?"

"I love it." I took it out of the box, admiring the way the diamonds sparkled even in the dim lighting of the bedroom. "Why did you get this for me?"

"There doesn't have to be a reason." He ran his finger along the bracelet before taking it from me and putting it on my wrist. "I wanted to do something special for you."

"Is this our new normal?"

"Do you want this to be our new normal?"

"I want whatever makes us happy and together."

I placed my palm on his cheek. "I don't ever want to be without you."

"I'll never leave you." He kissed me. "I don't think I'm capable of it."

He took the box and put it on the nightstand before turning off the light. "We can get a couple hours of sleep in before I have to go to my meeting." He laid down and pulled me into his chest. "I want to hold you."

"I like being held." I snuggled into his muscular chest, clasping my hand in his. "I like our new normal."

He was quiet for a few minutes, but he was still awake. I imagined that the conversation he had with Gio and the upcoming meeting with my uncle weighed heavily on his mind.

"What's today?" I asked.

"Thursday."

"No, I know that, but when you were on the phone with Gio, you told him you knew what day it was."

He was silent again.

"You don't have to tell me." I hugged him.

"It's our mother's birthday."

"Oh."

"She was a year older than I am now when she died." His body tensed as he tightened his hold on me. "She was murdered."

"I'm sorry." How horrible for him and Gio to be

so young and have to deal with that situation. "Do you know who did it?"

"There was never an investigation. There doesn't have to be when the person who murdered her had the police in his back pocket."

"But your father was so powerful. How did he let that happen... oh. He killed her."

"He was extremely abusive. They had such a toxic relationship. They'd fight, he'd hurt her, sometimes so bad that he'd send her away so she could heal from the attack."

"She must have been in so much anguish."

"She always forgave him. As a kid, I paid little attention to it. I wanted my family to be together. I hated when he sent her away. As an adult, I knew why she didn't leave him all together. My bastard father would never have let her leave with me and Gio. We were possessions to him. She stayed because of us."

"She wanted to protect you and Gio."

"She had no way out. She was a prisoner, just as much a possession as me and Gio. The night it happened, I think she was trying to leave. I remember seeing suitcases in the bedroom, but they mysteriously disappeared a few hours after her death."

"She died in the house?"

"In the bathroom," he lowered his tone. "I found her."

I sat up and took his hand in mine, trying to comfort him. He was tough on the outside, but these memories were with him every day.

"She was cold and alone. I don't know how long she'd been there before I went looking for her."

When he sat up, I crawled into his lap and rested my head on his shoulder.

"How old were you?"

"Eleven." He stroked my hair.

My heart broke for the little boy who walked in and found his mother that way. No wonder he had so many issues.

"He'd probably beaten her. Maybe she hit her head? I don't really know what happened. The official story was that she overdosed. Her family didn't believe that. They said she was leaving him. My father kept us away from her sisters and my grandmother. He wasn't going to let them poison us against him, but even at that young age, I knew he was responsible for her death. Even if she took too many pills and overdosed, he drove her to it."

"Romero, I can't imagine the pain and sadness this must have caused for you."

"It was a long time ago. I blocked a lot out. I had to look after Gio. He was only eight and I couldn't tell him how I'd found her. The pain on her face, even in death, will haunt me for the rest of my life. I hope she found peace because she had none when she was married to him."

"This is why you don't talk about her."

"Her name was Maria Elena," he said. "I don't talk about her because the memories are too dark. I'll never forget when they came and took her out of the house. I didn't want to let go of her hand, but they made me. I didn't cry because if she was watching me, I wanted her to see how strong I could be."

I wanted to be brave and comfort him, but I couldn't hold back the tears that insisted on wetting my cheeks.

"After my father was murdered, I took Gio, and we fled to Italy. I walked away from it all because I wanted nothing that had to do with my father's legacy. I didn't care who took it. I didn't want it."

"I understand why." I stroked his back.

"There were trusts set up for me and Gio. Giancarlo took care of all of that. We had money to live a very comfortable and entitled life. We could have gotten educations and become legitimate, but that wasn't in the cards for us."

"Why not?"

"When word got out that we were in Italy, people seemed to fear our last name. I used that to my advantage, so in the end, I used my father's connections to start my business, but I did it despite him. I let Antonio take everything my scum of a father worked for and I never avenged his death. I did that for my mother."

"You did the right thing."

"Some people saw me not avenging his death as a sign of weakness, but after I proved how resourceful and powerful I'd become in the organization without having any of the families backing me, most of my associates grew to respect me."

"But not the Torrios."

"No, not them."

"Does my uncle see you as a threat?"

"I never gave him a reason to come at me, but he did anyway." He twisted the ends of my hair around his finger. "We're going to resolve all of that this morning at the meeting."

"How do you know it isn't a trap?" The thought of Romero never coming home frightened me, but even worse, if his death was at the hands of my family, I could never forgive myself for my part in all of this.

"I don't."

"Then don't go." I held onto him. "Please, stay with me."

"Sweetheart, that's not the way this business works. I can't hide. I got myself into this sham alliance and I have to get myself out."

"What if they don't let you out? What if they hurt you, or worse?"

"There are procedures in place. They can't just take me or Gio out. We're protected by the organization because we're Bilottis. Some of the families still respect my father's reign."

"Someone took your father out."

"He had a lot of enemies and it was time for a regime change."

"I don't get how any of you can be part of such a brutal world."

"Most people don't." He shrugged. "It is what it is. I have to deal with the life I made."

"Is it really the life you want?"

"That's a question for another day." He kissed my temple. "I've opened up to you in ways I never thought I could."

"I appreciate that." I hugged him. "I want to understand you better. I want to know who you are."

"You know who I am." He took my face in his firm hold. "The same way I know who you are." He kissed me. "We belong together and no one is ever going to come between us."

A chill ran down my spine when I realized his words were a warning of things to come.

"That I can promise, Luciana."

CHAPTER 22

Romero

A light rain fell from the clouds as we walked up to the porch of the Torrio estate. I'd been to many funerals in my life. Today seemed like the kind of day we should bury someone. Maybe it was the weather. Maybe it was putting an end to this horrible business decision. Either way, I wanted all of this to be over. In a few hours, I could spend the rest of the day with my wife and forget this shitty situation ever happened.

All of my guys accompanied me to this meeting. Gio and I walked ahead of the entourage. Santino pulled up in his own car along with his guard and two of his brothers. If Antono tried something today, he would be viewed as reckless, and a man in his position couldn't appear that way in front of the other families.

"Are you ready for this?" Gio asked.

"I don't trust these people."

"You hit them hard last night. They're not going to let that go."

"I have a couple of ideas." I rang the doorbell. "We will walk out of her unattached to this family. It was a mistake to enter this alliance."

Rocco answered the door, looking like he hadn't slept all night. They were probably scrambling after their shipment was destroyed. They shouldn't have fucked with me.

"Hello Rocco," I greeted him.

"You should probably wipe that fucking grin off your face before you come inside." He looked over my shoulder. "Are all of them necessary?"

"You never know." I turned and looked at the small army behind us. "I like to be prepared."

"Dominick and Gianni Marchelli?" He sighed. "How did you get the Marchellis in your pocket?"

"I can assure you, Mr. Torrio," Santino approached the porch. "The Marchelli family cannot be bought. My brothers are here for security. They're going to ensure that the three of us walk out of here in one piece. My older brothers are very protective of me."

"No one can accuse you of being stupid, Bilotti." Rocco widened the door to let us in. "We're meeting in the study."

I followed the smug bastard down the hall, with Gio and Santino close behind me. As I took in the elaborate house with the ostentatious paintings and gold accents throughout the room, I took pleasure knowing that Luciana would never live here again. Her home was with me. No stupid alliance or lack thereof would dictate otherwise.

Antonio and Vincent waited for us in the study. Their stoic, pissed off faces alerted me they were not happy with my retaliation tactics. Fuck them.

"Mr. Bilotti," Antonio said. "Thank you for joining us."

"Torrio." I entered the room and took a seat across from his desk. HIs gaze followed my every move. Gio and Santino stood behind me as Rocco went to stand by his brother. Sandro was curiously absent from this meeting, and I wondered if that was by design.

"We have a problem." Antonio glared at me. "But I have a feeling you already know that."

"We've had a problem since the moment I entered into this alliance," I countered. "It's time for us both to admit we don't belong in business together."

"We may have entered this arrangement too hastily but I really thought you had inherited some of your father's skills."

"I have my own set of skills and they clearly don't line up with your business model." I glanced at Vincent and Rocco. "I can't work with people I don't trust."

"We can't work with people who blow up our shipments," Vincent said. "What do you think we should do about that?"

"I would find the person who betrayed you." I nodded. "Make them pay."

"I intend to." Antonio tapped his fingers on his desk.

"That's what I would do." *Don't think I won't make your family pay, old man.* "The thing is, you better make sure what you did to them doesn't come back to bite you."

"Why don't we cut the bullshit?" Vincent shouted. "We know it was you."

"Good luck proving that." Gio laughed. "I thought we were here to end this bullshit alliance."

"I have all the papers here." Santino handed them to Rocco. "Once these are signed it will undo any dealings the Torrios have with the Billioti organization."

"All the legal ones." Rocco took the file.

"It will be as if the other dealings never existed," I said. "It's not as if we got very far anyway. You murdered one of my lieutenants."

"You can't prove that." Vincent smirked at Gio.

"You sent me to work with the worst arms dealers I've ever encountered." *That's why those four idiots are dead.* "You stalled my merchandise, went behind my back with the cartel, and stuck the Feds on me."

The rage simmered to a boiling point inside my tense body when I thought of all the ways they tried to bring me down. The crazy thing was, I might have been able to forgive all of those things except for Arturo's death. One aspect of this whole shit show I would never forget was how they put Luciana in my path, knowing I would probably eliminate her if I found out about her part in all of this. I fell in love with my wife and that was the only thing that saved her. The Torrios didn't bank on that.

"You already had our father's territory," I said. "I didn't want it and I wasn't going to make a move on it. Why did you bother with this whole charade?"

"I believed it was beneficial for all of us." Antonio motioned around the room. "I thought by joining our families, we would become stronger."

Bullshit! That wasn't true, but I couldn't admit that without giving up Luciana. No matter how much I hated these people, I would never give them the satisfaction of knowing she failed their mission.

"You were already at the top of the food chain." I pointed at him. "You didn't need me, just my connections and my product. You've caused a great deal of aggravation for me with the Feds and the cartel."

"You answered back," Antonio said. "You took out that warehouse and shipment whether or not you admit to it. That took a lot of balls on your part."

"We do what we have to do." I stared into his soulless eyes, wondering how men like us became the way we were. "I'm willing to call all of this even and go back to the way things were before we joined forces."

"Are you sure about that?" Antonio asked. "Some things can't be undone."

"I don't see what can't be undone here." I stood and buttoned my suit jacket. "We put none of our business into motion. We did a lot of talking and mistrusting one another. This could have been a powerful alliance. One the other families would have respected."

"We already have their respect," Vincent said. "It's you who would have benefited from your union with us, which was why you agreed to it so quickly."

"I agree with Romero," Antonio said. "What I thought was going to be a fruitful relationship isn't going to work out after all."

"Once you sign those papers," Santino said. "All the legal dealings will be over. I'm sure we can all agree that means *everything*."

Just as we entered this alliance without putting anything illegal in writing, we were going to have to get out of it the same way. I'd have to trust these scumbags with no integrity one last time.

"There'll be no more retaliation?" Gio asked.

"As long as your organization doesn't encroach on our territory," Rocco said. "Although, now that our warehouse on the harbor is gone, it doesn't look like either of us will move anything for quite some time."

"With the Feds breathing down my neck and the cartel not trusting me, it doesn't look like I'll be encroaching on anything." I had to work on undoing what the Torrios had done to me. "I'm ready to go our separate ways, but I would like to know why you even bothered with this whole alliance."

I didn't expect Antonio to give me what I was looking for. If he answered me, he'd have to reveal that he never entered this agreement to form an alliance.

"I had a different vision when I offered you the union, but things change, and that's all I'm willing to say." He stood and extended his hand. "I hope you know there are no hard feelings. It's business."

I glanced down at his hand, wanting more than anything not to shake it. I'd much rather spit in his face, but if I wanted to buy myself some time, I needed to pretend I was fine with his explanation.

"Business." I shook his hand. "I trust you'll let me get on with mine."

I let go of his hand, nodded at Rocco and Vincent, and then turned and motioned for Gio and Santino to leave. As we made our way to the door, Antonio cleared his throat.

"We're not finished," Antonio said.

Of course we're not. This was all too easy.

"You have something that belongs to me."

"Fuck," Gio mumbled as I let out a frustrated breath.

"You cannot possibly mean my wife."

"No alliance," Antonio said. "No Luciana."

"Despite what you think." I slowly turned to face him, resisting the urge to reach for my gun and shoot him in the head. "Luciana is not a possession."

"You didn't think that when you married her," Rocco said. "When you came into this very room asking us to confirm if she was a virgin."

"Fuck off." I clenched my jaw. "My wife will never come back here."

"I can excuse a lot of things," Antonio said. "But I will not allow you to stay married to my niece. We'll have the arrangement annulled."

"Have you even asked Luciana what she wants?" I shouted. "Why would you? Have you ever considered her feelings once?"

"Like you do?" Rocco stepped toward me. "I've seen the social media posts. You're at that new club every night. Posing for pictures and fulfilling fantasies of women who would do anything to get into your bed."

"Romero would never do that to Luciana," Gio said. "He's committed to her."

"You don't have to explain anything to them." When I moved toward Antonio, both Rocco and Vincent stepped in front of me. "Luciana will not be coming back here. She is my wife in every sense of the word, despite our agreement. She has always been a disposable member of this family."

"That's not true," Rocco said.

"Can you really look me in the eye and tell me that with a straight face?" I asked.

"Let him have her," Vincent said. "She was never worth much to us, anyway."

"You son of a bitch." When I brought my hand back to punch him, Gio and Santino held me back. "Get off me!"

"It's time for us to go," Gio said. "Let's be done with these people."

"If you come for my wife." I broke out of Gio's hold. "All bets are off, and this peaceful resolution is over."

"Don't threaten me, Romero," Antonio said. "You may have clawed your way to the top using those tactics, but I can assure you, they won't work with me."

"I mean it, Torrio." I stared down at his sons. "If any of you come for Luciana, there will be hell to pay. That includes your wife."

"My wife?" Antonio looked as if I was telling him something new.

"Make sure you keep her away from Luciana." I headed for the door. "This concludes our business."

As we made our way to the front door, three large bodyguards followed us down the hall.

"We know our way out." I pushed open the door

and hurried out onto the porch. "Fuck!" I kicked the wall, looking for something to punch, but I didn't feel like breaking my hand on the bricks. "I hate this family."

"Calm down." Gio placed his hand on my shoulder. "We're free of them."

"Do you really think so?" I walked toward the car. "They're going to come for us."

"We'll be ready," Gio said. "They have no idea we know they were only in this to set us up. That's a huge advantage for us."

"We need to figure out how to shut them down."

"I'll see what I can find out," Santino said. "Like I said before, you have my family's full resources."

"We appreciate that." Gio shook Santino's hand. "We're probably going to need it."

"Have Giancarlo meet us at the house," I said. "I want answers and I want them today."

CHAPTER 23

*L*uciana

"Jag." I eagerly looked out the front windshield of the SUV. "How long before we get there?"

"Fifteen minutes, maybe," he said. "There's more traffic going into the city than I expected."

"I don't want to be late."

"Well, it's raining and you remember what happened last time it was raining?"

"How could I forget? I fell on my butt."

"I almost lost my job, possibly my life."

"Romero wouldn't kill you." My gaze connected with his in the mirror. "Would he?"

"I don't want to take any chances."

Sandro texted me about an hour ago and asked me to meet him at this new restaurant in the city. I hadn't heard from him in a few days, so when he said he wanted to have brunch, I jumped at the chance. My cousin and I used to spend a lot of time together. I wanted to tell him things had changed between me and Romero. I was in a real marriage and I was happy.

I had been anxious since Romero went to meet with my family this morning. I hadn't heard from him, and that worried me. Maybe Sandro could put me at ease.

"So, things are cool with you and the boss?" Jag asked. "I know it was a little tense when he was late for dinner last night."

"Late?" I giggled. "He missed it entirely."

"His loss was my gain."

"Things are good with us." My phone rang from inside my bag. "I think we're finally on the same page." I dug out my phone and saw that it was Romero. "Speak of the devil."

And, I mean devil.

"You better take that," Jag said. "He likes to know where you are."

"I've noticed." I accepted the call. "Hello."

"Where are you?" Romero asked.

"Don't you track my every move?" I laughed. "You tell me where I am."

"It looks like you're on your way into the city," he sighed. "Why would you be going to the city without me?"

"I'm meeting Sandro for brunch."

"What?" The tone of his voice was louder than I would have liked. "No, tell Jag to turn around."

"I will not."

"Luciana." If I were standing in front of him when he said my name, I'd be scared.

"Why are you so upset about me meeting Sandro? Did things not go well with my family?"

"They asked for you back."

"What?" I yelled. Jag glanced at me in the mirror. I held up my hand and waved, indicating everything was fine. "You can't be serious?"

"Don't worry, I'm not giving you back."

"Gee, thanks." I rolled my eyes. "How noble of you."

"I'm not in the mood," he said. "Come home. I have a bad feeling about this."

"I want to meet Sandro. The last time I saw him, he was unsettled. He probably needs to talk."

"Where are you headed? I'll meet you there."

"No."

"What?"

"I told you no."

"I heard you." He cursed under his breath in Italian.

"I know you don't like when I do that, but sometimes it can't be helped."

"Oh, I'll break you of that habit."

"Promises, promises." I smiled when I thought of

a few ways he could try and break me from telling him no.

"I'm serious, Luciana."

"Sandro wants to meet with me. If you show up, he'll be disappointed."

"If anything feels off, I want you to leave." He paused. "Put Jag on speaker."

"Why?"

"Just do it."

"Fine," I said. "Jag, my tyrant husband, wants to speak with you."

Jag nodded as I put Romero on speaker.

"Jag," Romero said. "Make sure Luciana gets back to me in one piece. Are we clear?"

"Yes, boss," Jag answered. "Nothing will happen to her."

"I'm not kidding," Romero warned. "If anything happens to her, this will be your last day on this earth."

"That's enough." I took Romero off speaker so Jag could focus on the road.

"I'll deal with you later," Romero said.

"I love you."

"I love you too, baby. Just be careful."

"Always." I ended the call as we drove down the street where I was meeting Sandro. "It's right up there." I pointed to the restaurant.

"There's nowhere to park." He pulled up in front

of the building behind the line of cars waiting for the valet. "We're going to have to use the valet service. I guess the rain is making everyone else valet too."

"Ok, you do that and I'll go meet Sandro."

"Lu, I'd feel better if I walked you in."

"Jag, you can watch me walk into the restaurant." I opened the door and slipped out of the car. "I'll be fine. I promise." I didn't wait for him to argue with me as I hurried under the awning of the restaurant to get out of the rain.

I wiped the raindrops from my face and entered the restaurant.

"Mrs. Bilotti," the hostess, who I didn't know, greeted me. "Your cousin is waiting for you."

"Oh, okay."

"Follow me," she said. "He's back here."

"Thank you." I followed her through the crowded dining area and to a back room. When she pulled open a sheer black curtain, I entered a small private area. There was only one table.

"Luciana." Vincent turned and faced me. "I'm so glad you could join me."

"Vincent." I looked around the room. "Where's Sandro?"

"He couldn't make it." He stood and motioned at the chair across from him. "Please, come join me."

"I don't understand." I sat down at the table, wondering why Sandro would set me up like this. "Why couldn't he make it?"

"He was busy, so I came in his place." He pointed to the glass in front of me. "I ordered you a mimosa. I know you like those with brunch."

"Thank you." I rested my hands in my lap, trying not to appear as uneasy as I felt. "How are you?"

"Good." He sipped his water. "You?"

"I can't complain." *Did Vincent know I had gone against the family and gave them false information?*

"Your husband is treating you well?"

"Yes." I picked up my glass and took a long sip of the cold orange juice mixed with a very smooth champagne. "Did your meeting with him go well today?"

"Not really."

"Oh." I took another gulp of my drink. "He's been pretty quiet with his business dealings lately."

"Has he?" He smiled at me. "I guess that's why you've had nothing for me these last few weeks."

"Ever since that issue with the Feds, he's been really careful." *Why am I talking so much?* "I mean, you know, he doesn't leave things around for me to see."

"We've ended our alliance." He waited as the server filled his water glass and brought me another mimosa. "Thank you, Gina."

"Can I get you anything else?" She bit her pouty bottom lip as she stared into his eyes.

What is it with these women and mobsters? I

finished my drink. *Who am I kidding? I'm one of those women.*

"In a few minutes." He touched her hand. "Let my cousin enjoy her mimosa."

"Maybe some bread or something," I said because I drank the first one too fast and now I needed some carbs.

"Of course," Gina said. "I'll be right back."

Vincent watched her leave the room before returning his attention to me.

"She's pretty." I wanted to talk about something other than Romero and the alliance.

"She is." He nodded. "As I was saying, the Torrios are no longer in business with Romero."

"Maybe that's a good thing." The room was spinning more than it should have. "I didn't drink that much."

"There's another drink right there." He motioned to my second glass. "If you're thirsty."

"No, I mean, there wasn't that much alcohol in the first drink, but I feel strange." My thoughts buzzed in my head, but I couldn't pick one thing to say. When I tried to stand, he placed his hands over mine.

"Sit down."

"I don't... I'm loopy." I took a sip of water, but I couldn't really focus. "I'm fine."

"Good."

"I was saying that maybe the end of the alliance

is for the best. The family never really wanted to be involved with Romero, anyway. I still don't understand why we went through all of this." My fingers tingled and my arms dropped like lead by my sides. "Where's the bread?"

"What's wrong, Lu?"

"I told you, I feel strange."

"I wonder why."

"Huh?"

"So, why don't you tell me what you've been up to with your new husband?"

"What do you mean?"

"This is really nice." He tugged on my new bracelet. "It looks expensive."

"Romero gave it to me."

"What did you have to do to get that?" He smirked. "I can only imagine."

"I need to leave." Romero was right. This was a bad idea. "I have to go."

"I don't think so, Lu." He moved his chair closer to mine and held onto my arm, keeping me in place. "We're going to have a little chat."

"About what?"

"How you betrayed your family."

"No, I did everything you asked me to do." I shook my head, pushing back the anxiety. "But it's never enough. I was never enough for any of you."

"Is that why you betrayed us?"

"I-I didn't..." My head wouldn't stop spinning. "I didn't mean to."

"What happened to the plan?"

"Romero figured it out." I drank some more water, hoping it would help the flash of heat that engulfed me. "What was in that drink?"

"Let's not worry about that right now." He grabbed my wrist. "Tell me what you did?"

"I didn't do anything."

"You're lying." He squeezed my arm. "You're going to be sorry for what you've done."

"I want to go home now."

"You're going home," he said. "With me."

"No, I'm going back to Romero." I struggled out of his hold. "Let go of me or I'll cause a scene."

"Do you think anyone in this place that I own, I might add, is going to question me?" He yanked me toward him. "Poor, stupid, naïve Lu. I knew you didn't have the stomach for this. I know you'd fuck it up."

"I didn't fuck anything up," I shouted. "Romero figured it out because he's smarter than you."

"If he's so smart, why would he let his wife come and meet with one of us?"

"He thought I was meeting with Sandro."

"I sent the text asking you to meet me. Alessandro isn't even in the country." He laughed. "Your husband should have known that. He should have made sure you were safe, but I guess he doesn't care about you either."

"He does." I tried to stand, but I fell back into my chair. "What did you do to me?"

"A mild sedative." He grabbed my bag and took out my phone. "You'll be asleep by the time we get to the car."

"You jerk."

"We're going to leave your phone here since I know your husband tracks your every move."

"My guard will never let me leave with you."

"Your incompetent guard? The one who let you walk in here unattended? The same one who hasn't checked on you? Do you think Sam would ever have been so reckless with you?"

"Jag was valeting the car." I tried to take my phone from him, but he tossed it in the corner of the room. "He thought I was meeting Sandro."

"Your guard. Your husband. Your family." He stood and pulled me out of my chair. "No one cares about you."

"Let me go." I shoved at his chest. "I'm not going with you."

"You don't have a choice." He wrapped his arm around my waist. "We're going out the back. My guard is in the alley waiting with my car. Jag is upstairs, standing outside of a room he thinks you're in. I made sure the hostess took him there. Romero will probably kill him for this. I know I would."

"You bastard."

"We can do this the easy way." He dragged me through the doorway. "Or I can pick you up and carry you out."

"I don't want to go with you." I shouted. "Jag!"

"He can't hear you and anyone who can wouldn't dare cross me."

"Please, help me!" I tried to yell louder, but the music and the conversation from the patrons drowned out my pleas.

"You've had too much to drink." He pulled me closer to his side. "I'm just getting you home safely."

"Why are you taking me back home?" My eyes were heavy, but I fought to keep them open. "None of you want me there."

"We need you there."

"Why?"

"If we take you, your husband will start a war." When we stepped out into the alley, the cool rain pelted against my face. "If he comes at us, we can take him out. The council won't question it."

"You want to..." I stiffened my stance and tried to prevent him from getting me into the SUV. "You want to kill him?"

"He'll lose his mind when he realizes we took you." My legs buckled as he opened the car door. "He thinks you're a possession."

"No, I'm his wife."

"He'll come for you and when he does, we'll defend ourselves."

He shoved me into the backseat and slammed the door. My eyes drifted shut as I slumped against the door, too tired to fight back.

Romero...

CHAPTER 24

Romero

I sat in my office with Gio and Giancarlo. It was time to figure out how to oust Torrio from power. That was the only way for me to run my product into New York.

"Two more families have sided with you since the warehouse bombing," Giancarlo said. "Your show of strength puts them in your corner."

"With those two families and the Marchellis backing." Gio slapped his hand on his thigh. "That gives us the majority."

"Torrio is still the head family," I reminded him. "There's only one way to undo that."

"Someone has to take him out." Giancarlo gazed out the window. "There hasn't been a regime change in a long time. Not since your father was in charge. I don't think anyone would take that risk."

"Things have been different for a while," I said. "The families have been working peacefully for years. They have been coexisting and as long as no one oversteps, everyone is happy."

The mafia had to learn to adapt and change in recent years. With cameras on every street corner and the internet making us all famous, we had to learn to co-exist or there would be no business for any of us.

"What changed all of that?" Gio asked. "Why did they come for the Bilottis?"

"Old vendettas," Giancarlo suggested. "When Antonio approached me with the alliance, I thought it was a good opportunity for you. I never would have brought it to you if I thought he was going to doublecross you. I wouldn't disrespect your father that way."

Why is he apologizing for this now?

"I thought you could work with them." Giancarlo continued. "In a few years, when Antonio wanted to step away, there would be enough territory for you and his sons to run a major empire. Between their connections in the city and your international associates, you would have it all."

"The Torrios were not on the same page," Gio said. "They wanted everything Romero and I built. If we hadn't figured out Lu was a plant, they might have succeeded."

"I'm sorry your wife betrayed you." Giancarlo frowned. "Such a sign of disrespect."

"It wasn't her fault," I raised my voice. "She is a victim of all of this."

"Of course," Giancarlo said. "I meant no disrespect."

"We have another issue that we've been investigating." I glanced at Gio. "We've been sitting on it, but I think it could be useful if we had some background information. You might be just the man who could help us figure out what we have and how we can use it."

"I'll help you anyway I can," Giancarlo said. "What do you need?"

I opened the drawer in my desk and took out the file with Lu's parents' report in it. "This has been bothering me for a few weeks." I handed him the folder. "This report was buried deep. Luciana's parents did not die in a car accident."

Giancarlo read over the file. He didn't look surprised, but I figured he wouldn't.

"There was tension between my father and Antonio before he died. What was going down around the time of Lu's paren's' deaths?"

"It was a long time ago, but I remember some ramblings. Gossip even." He shook his head. "We were running a much different organization back then. We didn't question personal problems or rumors that didn't involve the business."

"Antonio's sister and her husband were executed before that car crashed."

Giancarlo continued to read the file, but at some point, he must have stopped reading because I had lost him in an old memory. He rubbed his temple and stared out the window.

"Giancarlo?" I asked. "What do you remember from this accident?"

"I haven't thought about this in years," he said.

"Antonio would not have buried this report, so who fucking did?"

My patience was wearing thin.

"Torrio wouldn't, but your father would."

"Why?" I asked.

"Because your father killed Lu's parents."

Fuck!

"What?" Gio yelled. "Why?"

"There were rumors and gossip, but back then we didn't have social media and people taking pictures every three minutes." He shook his head, looking disgusted. "Your generation ruined our business dealings."

"What were the rumors?" I asked. "Why did my father kill Lu's parents?"

"I don't know the full story, but there was an affair years earlier. It had the potential to blow things up in ways that no one wanted." Giancarlo got up from his chair and stood behind it. "We were dealing with a new attorney general who vowed to take down organized crime. Your father didn't need any distractions."

"What affair?" I asked.

"Your father and Kristina Torrio," he said.

"No fucking way," Gio said. "He slept with her? There's no accounting for taste, is there?"

"They were on and off for many years," Giancarlo said. "It was over years before Lu's parents were killed. I thought they had ended things before you were born, Gio."

"What do Lu's parents have to do with an old affair?" I tried to make sense of this situation. "They were killed years after Gio was born. If the affair was over, then why would our father murder them?"

"I'm not really sure." Giancarlo gripped the back of the chair. "Does it really matter?"

"Yes," I shouted, because I didn't like his dismissive attitude. "My father is responsible for killing my wife's parents. I need to know why?"

"Leave it buried," Giancarlo said. "It's not useful information. It can't help you."

"Tell me what else you know and let me decide," I demanded. "Think hard, old man, because you got us into this fucking mess."

"I was trying to help you realize your birthright," he raised his voice. "Do you know how disappointed your father would be to know it has taken you this long to take your rightful place among the families?"

"What does any of that have to do with Luciana's

parents? Do you think I need my father's approval?" I pounded my fist on the desk. "Finish the fucking story."

"That woman is going to bring you down," he mumbled. "Both of you."

"What did you just say?" I gritted my teeth. "That's my wife you're talking about."

"Let's calm down," Gio said. "Giancarlo, do you remember any reason our father would put a hit out on Lu's parents?"

"Luciana's mother, Stefania, found out about the affair. I don't know why we're rehashing this now?"

"Because it's important to me," I said.

"Kristina and Stefania were very close," Giancarlo tightened his grip on the chair. "Like sisters."

"Seriously?" I shook my head. "Kristina hates Luciana. If she was so close to Stefania why does she treat her daughter the way she does?"

"I don't know their history, but I know they were out one night and Kristina had too much to drink. Your father and I had to retrieve them because his name was being thrown around and there were people in there who could cause problems if they had the wrong information." Giancarlo waved his hand as he spoke. "Kristina confided in Stefania, thinking because they were so close she would keep her secret."

"But Stefania wouldn't betray her brother by keeping that secret," Gio said. "Kristina told our father that she had let the affair slip to Lu's mother."

Giancarlo nodded.

"He had them killed," Gio said. "To keep a secret of an old affair? That doesn't make sense."

"Kristina didn't want Antonio to find out," Giancarlo confirmed. "There was already so much tension between the two families. Antonio was rising to power faster than your father would have liked."

"But he killed Antonio's sister," Gio said.

"As I said, I didn't know all the details, but I hired the hitman because that's what I did." He looked at my brother. "Just as you do Gio, you do whatever Romero tells you because you would do anything for him as I would have done anything for your father. No questions asked."

"What else would you do for our father?" I asked.

"What do you mean?" Giancarlo squinted at me.

"How far would you take that loyalty?" I ran my hand along my jaw, cursing myself for not seeing this before. "It was always you."

"What are you talking about?" Giancarlo straightened his stance. "What are you saying?"

"You brought this alliance to me because you knew I trusted you." I didn't even question it. I had no reason to. "You set me up."

"Romero?" Gio yelled.

"No, Gio." I held up my hand to stop him. "You didn't trust that alliance, but you trusted me to make the right decision. I fucked this whole thing up, but I didn't do it by myself, did I?"

"What are you accusing me of?" Giancarlo asked. "I aligned you with a powerful family. That same family that has your father's territory."

"You put me in a position of weakness," I shouted. "All because I didn't avenge my father's death. I didn't take his territory. You never accepted that I didn't want it."

"How could I accept it? Everything Mario built you spit on when you walked away. He's turning in his grave." He motioned between me and Gio. "Do you think Dante Marchelli or Antonio Torrios' sons would leave their father's death unanswered?"

"Our father isn't worth the time." I picked up the glass on my desk and threw it against the wall. "He was a piece of shit and I have no interest in avenging him. He's where he belongs for what he did to our mother."

"You ungrateful son of a bitch." Giancarlo motioned around my study. "The only reason you have any of this is because of the sacrifices your father made. He was a vigorous leader. He worked to build an empire for you and Gio, but neither of you had the balls to claim it."

"Giancarlo," Gio said. "You're out of line."

"I'm tired of watching the two of you disrespect the legacy your father left." He paced the room. "You are entitled and spoiled. You always have been."

"You thought by aligning us with Antonio we would finally take over the territory we never wanted?" I asked. "Something isn't right."

When I looked at Gio, he nodded in agreement with me.

"Does any of it matter now?" Giancarlo asked. "You screwed this alliance up from the beginning. You were so taken by your new bride, you didn't even see what she was doing. I thought once you realized they were setting you up, you would come at them and take what was rightfully yours, but you couldn't do it."

"You knew Antonio's plan from the beginning," Gio said. "You put Romero in a deadly situation and now he could lose everything we built."

"I put Romero in the perfect situation." He clenched his jaw. "Your brother was too stupid to see what was right in front of him. He didn't act as ruthless as I thought he would. He didn't take control soon enough. He failed miserably."

"You set me up." My body shook with a fury I hadn't felt since the day I realized my father was the one who took my mother from me. "You don't think I'm ruthless enough?"

"I did what I had to do to avenge your father," he said. "The two of you would never take your rightful place without that alliance. You needed a push, and I gave it to you. When Antonio came to me with his plan, I realized it had to be done. You were going to sink or swim. I figured you would get exactly what you deserved. If you were strong, you would have it all, but you don't have that kind of ambition. I have no regrets. I told you I would do anything for your father."

"You knew what they were making Luciana do, and you didn't come to me?" His betrayal knew no bounds.

"Fuck, Luciana!" Giancarlo yelled. "You're missing the whole point. That must be some pussy."

When Giancarlo laughed, something inside me snapped.

"I'm so ashamed of the failure you've become. You're nothing like the man your father was."

"You're right." I drew my gun from the back of my pants. "I'm a hell of a lot worse."

"Romero." Giancarlo held up his hands when he realized what I meant, but it was too late. I pulled the trigger faster than his reflexes could cover his face, firing that bullet right between his eyes and sending him straight to hell.

"Fuck." Gio looked down at his blood-spattered shoes. "I just bought these."

"I guess he was wrong about me."

"I'd say so, you ruthless bastard."

"I had to do it," I said. "He betrayed us and don't tell me he was doing it for the right reasons. We didn't do things the way he wanted, so he almost destroyed everything we worked for. He was a liability we didn't need."

"I agree." Gio made the sign of the cross and said a silent prayer as Joey and Salvi came barreling in with their guns drawn.

"We're fine," I said. "But I'm going to need you to take care of this." I pointed to Giancarlo's body. "Before Lu gets home."

"Right away," Joey said.

"Quickly and discreetly," Gio warned. "Or you'll be next."

Gio and I left the study, closing the door behind us.

"I'm glad you're nothing like dad," Gio said.

"You don't think I'm going to kill my wife anymore?"

"Uh, well considering you just blew Giancarlo's brains out defending her honor, I'd say, I think you're going to let her live. Dad would never have defended mom that way." He put his arm around me. "Let's be serious. You shot him because he disrespected Lu."

"That was a big part of it," I agreed. "He was a liability, but when that old fuck spoke about her that way, I didn't hesitate."

As we walked down the hallway, Jag came through the front door, out of breath, soaking wet, and looking more distressed than I would have liked. *Why is he alone?*

"Mr. Bilotti," he said.

"Where is Luciana?" I fought the urge to reach for my gun, but if he didn't give me an answer I wanted to hear, Giancarlo's body wouldn't be the only one we'd be burying tonight.

"I... I don't know, sir."

CHAPTER 25

Luciana

"I found out I have a traitor in my house." Romero gripped my throat in his hand. "What should I do about that?"

There was no way out of this now. It was too late. I should have been the one to tell him what I had done.

"Luciana, do you know who the traitor is?"

I nodded as the tears flowed down my cheeks.

"I want to hear you say it," he shouted. "If you're brave enough to come into my house and betray me, you should be able to admit it."

"It was me," I cried. "But I didn't want to do it."

"You didn't want to do it?" When he tightened the grip on my throat, I prayed he would kill me quickly. "What the fuck does that mean?"

"Please." I tugged at his hand, but he didn't release his hold on my neck. "Stop."

He climbed on top of me, pinning me down. His reck-

less gaze held no emotion. He would never understand why I had done this. He wasn't wired that way. There was only one way for him to deal with betrayal. I couldn't even explain why I did it.

His hold was so tight around my throat that my eyes bulged. I gasped for air when he let go of me, but I didn't dare move. He wasn't finished with me.

"Give me one fucking reason why I shouldn't snap your neck and send you back to your uncle in a body bag?"

"Because." The words came out before I had time to process them. "I love you."

"You love me?" His laughter made me feel insignificant. "What the hell am I supposed to do with that?"

"Maybe not laugh at me and let me explain."

"The floor is all yours, butterfly."

He got off me and removed his gun out of the back of his pants and placed it on the desk, reminding me I wasn't fast enough to run out of here.

"You're running out of time," he said. "I'm all out of patience when it comes to you."

"I didn't want to do any of this," I admitted. "I didn't want to marry you, but they told me I had to. They told me this was an assignment, but I had no idea how far in I would become. I didn't expect to like you, let alone fall for you."

"So, you're telling me they made you do this. They didn't give you a choice?"

"Not at all." If I had a choice, did he think I would

have done it? "They told me they needed to know if they could trust you before working with you. I was supposed to spy on you and make sure you weren't betraying them."

"That doesn't make any sense. There would be no reason for me to betray them. They approached me."

"I didn't know any of that. I trusted what they said, but I realized soon after that they wanted me to bring them information about you and your business. They weren't trying to gauge your trust. They were trying to bring you down."

He said nothing, but it didn't look as if he believed me.

"I thought about running, but where would I go? They would find me, and once I became your wife, I couldn't leave. You would have come after me too. I was stuck in a horrible situation. I couldn't say no to my family, but I couldn't pretend to be your wife either."

"What do you mean?"

"Our wedding night was real for me." *When he made love to me, I believed we had a connection. One that might withstand my family.* "Why do you think I was so mad at you the next day? You left me alone and vulnerable. I had no idea how to process what we had done. I needed you to stay with me that night. And then, you took me to that business meeting and made me watch as you killed two people. I was terrified of you, but I had to stay and do what my family asked of me."

"You could have come to me. I would have protected you."

"The same way my family protects me? I hate them for thinking they could put me in this situation and expect me to be with you as your wife and not develop feelings for you. They made me betray you and I let them."

"You didn't give me a chance, Luciana." He dropped to his knees in front of me, taking me by surprise. *"I told you on our wedding day, I wanted to try to make this real, but you had no intentions of ever doing that."*

"I was too afraid."

When I touched his face, he moved back, stunned by my actions. His rejection knocked the wind out of me. I wanted more than anything for him to tell me he believed me. That he loved me too, but he admitted something I didn't know was possible.

"You fucking hurt me."

I opened my eyes, disoriented and groggy. My old bedroom? *How did I get here?* I pushed myself into a seated position, but the pounding behind my eyes forced me back into the pillows.

The rain smashed against the skylight above my head. Brunch, Sandro, not Sandro. I closed my eyes and tried to focus. Jag parked the car, and I went into the restaurant. *Vincent!* I slipped out of the bed, looking around for my shoes.

"Romero." The churning in my stomach intensified when I realized he was going to think I left him.

I would never hurt him the way I did before. Would he trust that? Would he know I was here?

I frantically searched the bedroom, but my shoes and bag weren't there. The old landline that I hadn't used in years was no longer plugged into the phone jack.

I needed to get out of here. When I yanked open the door, Vincent and Rocco were waiting on the other side.

"What the hell?" I jumped back, startled by their presence.

"Good, you're awake," Vincent said.

"I brought you something to eat and some water." Rocco followed Vincent into the bedroom with a tray of food. "You must be hungry."

"I'm not eating anything you give me." I glared at Vincent. "He drugged me."

"You drank too much." Vincent took a seat on the pink loveseat by the closet. "I had to carry you out of the restaurant. It was really embarrassing."

"You're a liar!" I shouted. "I'm leaving."

"You could try," Vincent said. "But you know Rocco and I are faster and stronger."

"Lu." Rocco placed the tray on the end table. "Sit down and eat. I wouldn't put anything in your food."

"Don't act like you care about me." I sat on the edge of the bed because there was nowhere for me to go in my bare feet, anyway. "Why am I here?"

"It was time for you to come home." Vincent tapped the arm of the chair.

"My home is with Romero."

"Not anymore," he said. "That's over and done with."

"That's not for you to decide." I jumped up and stomped to the window. "I don't belong here. I never have."

"Lu," Rocco sighed. "Things are going to get intense and dangerous. You were never meant to be with Bilotti forever. It's over. You're not going back to him."

"Do you think I'm going to accept that?" I pointed at Rocco. "Do exactly what you say?"

"Yes, Luciana, I do." Rocco's icy gaze studied me. "That's how it works. You served your purpose. You did what we asked and now it's unnecessary for you to be there anymore."

"Not to mention, you betrayed us," Vincent said. "Romero has known what we were up to for a few weeks. How do you suppose that happened?"

"That wasn't my fault." Didn't we already have this conversation? The memory was fuzzy, but at the restaurant, Vincent told me his plan. "You want Romero to come for me?"

"I'm counting on it," Vincent smirked. "No one in any of the other families will blame the Torrios for protecting their home and their family. Actually, little cousin, you're the key to this entire plan."

"How do you figure?" I asked.

"Because when that animal comes for you and I shoot him in the head." He stood and faced me. "We're going to tell everyone you left him and he couldn't handle that. He lost it and we did what we had to do to protect what was ours."

"I'm not yours." I gritted my teeth. "I want nothing to do with this family."

"You ungrateful little bitch." Vincent advanced to me, backing me against the wall. "We have taken care of you your whole life. We asked you to do one thing, and you fucked it up beyond repair."

"Take care of me?" Was he out of his mind? "I have been a throwaway member of this family since the day I arrived. Do you know what it's like to be an outsider looking in? How hard I tried to be part of this family, even when no one wanted me?"

"Lu," Rocco said. "Was it really that bad? You got an education, more money than most people see in a lifetime, and you grew up in a big house with all the luxuries most people would die for."

"If people knew what kind of family this really is, no one would be dying to become part of it." I didn't want to hurt Rocco. In some ways, he was a victim too. Being Antonio's son messed him up just as much as Romero's father had screwed him up. None of them had a chance. "Please forget this vendetta you have against Romero. You probably don't even know why you're fighting with him. Let me go back to him. We can stop whatever this is."

"Stop living in a fantasy world," Vincent said. "You're as much a part of this as the rest of us. The only difference between us is that I'm not a whore."

"Vincent," Rocco said.

"No, she should know what we think about her. How she totally fucked up this plan. We sent you in there to do a job, but you fell for the mark. All you had to do was not get caught."

"I had to do a little more than that." I had to trick my husband into believing I was there in good faith. When he found out about my betrayal, I had to stay alive. My so-called family didn't care about any of that.

"We know." Vincent shook his head. "Don't act like you didn't enjoy that part. Is that how he got you to turn on us? To leak false information? Do you know how you made the Torrios look when you fed us that bogus bullshit?"

"Maybe if you were the big, important mobster you want everyone to believe you are," I said. "You would have verified the information before you sent the Feds in to raid a legal shipment. If you look like fools in front of the other families, it's because you are."

"I'd watch your mouth, little girl," he said. "Once we kill your husband, we're all you're going to have left.If you don't get back on my good side, no one will protect you from my mother."

"Do you honestly believe I would stay here and take any more of her abuse?" I looked between him and Rocco. "From any of you? I'm done. Romero will never walk into your trap. He's smarter than you'll ever be when it comes to this business."

"He's an uneducated thug who made his way into this world by lying, cheating, and stealing. Your husband wasn't even honorable enough to avenge his father's death. He's a lowlife who deserves a disloyal, ungrateful bitch like you."

"Screw you." I hauled my hand back and slapped his cheek harder than I've ever hit anything in my life. It was the most satisfying thing I'd ever experienced. The sting in my palm was worth it.

Vincent retaliated, the force of his hand connecting with my cheek propelled me backward. I landed on my backside, stunned. The sting in my palm was nothing compared to the hit to my face.

My hand trembled as I pressed it against my cheek. I gazed up at Vincent just as he was coming toward me, but Rocco intervened.

"What the fuck is wrong with you?" Rocco pushed his brother back. "She's a woman and family."

"She deserved it for betraying us." Vincent looked down at me. "I was going to spare you, Lu, when I killed him, but now you're going to watch.

The last face your husband will see is the woman who caused his death. The one who claimed to love him." He backed out of the room. "Think about that."

"Please, Rocco." I used the edge of the bed to get into a standing position. "Don't let them do this."

He closed the door without saying anything, leaving me alone and defenseless against them. My only hope was that the man I trusted would come for me. But if he did, he'd die.

How could I live my life without Romero?

CHAPTER 26

Romero

"What do you mean, you don't know?" I grabbed Jag by the throat and shoved him against the door. "Where is my wife?"

"She went into the restaurant while I parked the car," he explained. "I wasn't gone that long."

"You let her go in by herself?" I pulled him to me and then shoved him hard into the door, hitting his head against the heavy wood. "I told you not to let her out of your sight."

"I'm sorry, I…"

"You're sorry." I hauled my arm back and punched him in the face. The thought of him being so careless with her unleashed a wrath that could not be contained. When he fell to the floor, I kicked him in his side. "Get up, you worthless piece of shit." I kicked him again. "Why is it so difficult for you to protect her? It's your only fucking job."

"Okay." Gio held me back. "That's enough."

"Get up," I yelled at my useless guard. "I trusted you with the most important job."

"I know, and I'm really sorry."

"Stop saying that," I shouted.

"Let's concentrate on finding Lu." Gio said as Jag struggled to get on his feet. Blood poured from his nose and he wobbled side to side. If I didn't need to focus on finding Luciana, he would be dead by now. "If I let go of you are you going to go after Jag again?"

I pushed Gio off me. "Tell me what happened," I said to Jag. "Don't leave anything out. I'll decide after if you're going to live."

"When I got into the restaurant," he stopped to catch his breath but that only made me want to hit him again. "The hostess brought me upstairs to a private room and told me Lu was in there with Sandro, so I waited, but she never came out."

"So, you don't know if she was actually in there?" Gio checked his phone.

"Which is why you don't let her go places alone," I shouted. "What is wrong with you?"

"How long were you waiting for her?" Gio asked.

"Not long. Maybe an hour," Jag said. "I thought she was eating and visiting with Sandro."

"I don't pay you to think." I called Lu's phone, but it went straight to voicemail.

"According to the tracker," Gio said. "Her phone

is still at the restaurant. Are you sure she wasn't there?"

"When they finally let me into the room, it wasn't being used at all. She was never there."

"Why didn't you call me as soon as you realized she was missing?" I shouted. "What's wrong with you?"

"I-I panicked."

"You fucking panicked?" There was no way I would let him live. "If anything happens to her…"

"They probably took Lu out the back before Jag even got into the restaurant," Gio said. "And paid the valet to delay him."

"Get someone at that restaurant. I need answers." I looked through my contacts. "I'm calling Sandro and telling that motherfucker he has fifteen minutes to get her back here before I kill all of them."

"Hey," Sandro answered. "Romero?"

"Where is Luciana?" I yelled. "Put her on the phone right now."

"Dude, I'm not with her."

"Where is she?"

"How should I know?"

"You had brunch with her and she never came home. Her guard can't find her."

"Wait, I didn't have brunch with her," he said.

"What do you mean? You texted her and asked her to meet you in the city."

"No, I didn't."

"If you're fucking around with me, I swear to god I'll kill you." I took a deep breath. "Where is my wife?"

"Romero, I'm not even in the country, so I couldn't have met Lu today," he said. "I'm in Portugal on a much needed vacation."

"You're not with her?"

"I don't know why she told you she was with me, but check my social media if you don't believe me. I got here yesterday." He paused for a moment. "Is it possible my cousin left you?"

"No, she wouldn't do that." Maybe a month ago she would have, but I was certain, especially after last night and this morning, she wouldn't do that to me. "Thanks for nothing."

I ended the call.

"Well?" Gio asked.

"He says he's in Portugal."

"Why would Lu say she was meeting him?" Gio scrolled through his phone.

"Because she believed she was."

"Sandro isn't lying." He turned the screen of his phone to face me. "He's not in this country."

"Why are you still here?" I glared at Jag. "In case you didn't figure it out, you're fucking fired. Get out of here before I kill you." There was no guarantee I wasn't going to kill him.

"I want to stay and help find her," he said.

"Get the fuck out of here." I looked at Gio. "If he's not out of my sight in three seconds…"

"Jag, leave us alone for a while," Gio said. "Romero is showing a remarkable amount of restraint by not beating you to death, so count your blessings and leave."

Jag went out the front door without a fight. Maybe he wasn't as stupid as I thought.

"He fucked up," Gio said. "We'll deal with him."

"It's not entirely his fault." I punched the wall, busting right through the sheetrock. "I should have had more guys on her. I shouldn't have let her go. I could have gone with her."

"We can't deal with what we didn't do." Gio leaned against the door. "We have to focus on getting her back. "

"We know where she is."

"Look, I have to ask," Gio said. "Are you sure she didn't leave willingly?"

"Seriously?" Why did everyone think Luciana would walk out on me?

"Things haven't been perfect between the two of you."

"Were they ever?" I sat on the bottom stair. "We have issues."

"Last night was intense." He waved his hand around the room. "Maybe she decided it was too much."

"Everything was fine between the two of us.

Better than it's ever been. I told her I loved her and I wanted to marry her for the right reasons." I shook out my swollen hand. "She didn't leave me. She wouldn't do that."

"I believe you."

"I'm losing control." I got up and pointed down the hall. "Giancarlo is dead, my business is going downhill by the minute, and the Torrios have Luciana."

"I'll admit that things have gotten out of control over the last few hours. I mean, we didn't even discuss Dad sleeping with Kristina."

"That's fucked up and disgusting."

"Do you think we can use it?"

"If Antonio doesn't already know, it would be a good way to get back at Kristina for the way she's treated Lu all these years. And all because she was pissed because Stefania wanted to tell her brother about Kristina's affair."

"I'd like to hear the rest of that story," Gio said.

"It is all so messed up, but I have a feeling I may have eliminated Giancarlo too fast. He might have had more information."

"He was too interested in us taking over Torrios territory to remember an affair that happened years ago. It is strange that Dad would kill Antonio's sister and her husband over an affair. Let's face it. He wasn't worried about Mom's feelings, and she was already gone by the time Lu's parents were killed.

Why would he kill them and cover it up? Did Kristina mean that much to him?"

"If you ask me, they deserved one another." I didn't have time to think about any of that. "We'll decide later if it's anything we can use, but right now, we need a plan to get Luciana back home."

"We know how to get into the Torrio estate undetected. We've done it before."

We had scoped out the house before the engagement party, making sure there would be no surprises. We found an old wine cellar that connected to the house underground. It led to a door in the basement that was long forgotten. Once inside that door, we were in the house. But getting in was the easy part. Getting past the guards was another story.

"Their security will be on high alert," I said. "We're going to need all the manpower we can find."

"I'll get on it, but we all can't storm the gate. That will be a bloodbath, for sure." Gio ran his hand through his hair. "It will put Lu in the crossfire."

"That can't happen. No matter what, Gio, she has to be protected."

"I know, man."

"I'll be the one to go in and get her."

"Alone?"

"I can get past the guards by myself. I know where her room is."

"They'll be expecting you." He tightened his jaw. "I don't like it."

"Here's something else you're not going to like." I didn't want to think about this, but it had to be said. "If something happens to me I need a favor."

"Don't say that."

"Shut up and let me finish." I placed my hand on his shoulder. "I'll protect Luciana at all costs. I would give up my life for hers."

"It won't come to that."

"The Torrios are wild cards. I still don't know why they came after us, and at this point, I don't care. I only want Lu out of there. If something should happen to me, promise me you will take care of her. You'll make sure those people don't hurt her anymore than they already have."

"Romero, I don't..."

"Listen to me." I gripped his shoulder. "I don't have an updated will. When we married, I should have provided for her. Everything I have goes to you."

"Stop this." He held my gaze. "This is unnecessary."

"Promise me, you'll take care of Luciana if it comes to that. Give her whatever she wants." Not that she would ever ask Gio for anything. "Make sure she goes to law school. Make sure she's happy, okay?"

"Do you want me to marry her too?"

"I'll fucking come back from the grave and rip your balls off if you marry her." I let go of his shoulder. "Just promise me."

"Fuck, I promise, but it's not gong to come to that."

"You're an amazing second, you know that?"

"I'm better than amazing, but yeah, I know." He took out his phone. "Are we done with all this mushy bullshit because I have an extraction to organize? If we're going to get her out of there, we're going to need a ton of support."

"Let's go get my girl."

CHAPTER 27

Luciana

As I stared out the window, I grew more anxious. The rain had stopped an hour ago, but I was no closer to figuring out how to get out of here. If I couldn't leave, I had to warn Romero not to come for me. He would walk into a trap. One that I wouldn't be able to protect him from.

I couldn't sit in this room and wait for my family to ambush him when he arrived. I could go to them and tell them there was no reason to go to war. We could tell Romero I wanted to stay here, and he didn't have to come for me. If that would protect him, I would do it. I was reaching, because the whole reason for Vincent forcing me to be here was for them to have an excuse to kill Romero. I had to try something.

I opened the bedroom door and peeked out. Thankfully, no one was waiting for me on the other side. I didn't expect them to be guarding me, considering I couldn't just walk out the front door. I still didn't have any shoes, no phone, purse, and no money. Not to mention the guards at the front of the property wouldn't allow me to get very far. Once a prisoner, always a prisoner.

My heart rate increased when I made my way down the hall. I had no idea where I was headed and what I would say once I got there, but I couldn't sit in that room and be a victim for one more second. If they were going to kill Romero, they'd have to kill me too. Let them try explaining that to the other families.

As I turned the corner, someone grabbed me from behind and pulled me into the out cove. Before I could scream, they cupped my mouth with their hand. I struggled, kicking backward and connected with their muscular legs.

"Whoa, my little butterfly." Romero turned me to face him, removing his hand from my mouth. When he smiled at me, all of my fear slipped away. Those gorgeous eyes, sexy grin, and stunning mouth took away all of my anxiety.

"Oh, God!" I wrapped my arms around his neck and hugged him as hard as I could. "You're here."

"Where else would I be?" He pressed his lips to mine, kissing me deeply and holding me close. "I'd lose my mind without you."

"When I woke up here, all I could think about

was what you were going through. How you must have thought... I didn't leave you," I said. "They took me against my will."

"I was ninety-nine percent sure that was true, but on my way in here, I thought maybe I would have to kidnap you."

"You're rescuing me." I kissed him. "I would never leave you. I love you."

"I love you too, but we need to get out of here."

I held onto him, never happier to see him, until I remembered how much danger he was in. What Vincent would do to him if they found him?

"What happened to your face?" He gently ran his finger over my swollen cheek. "Who did this?"

"It's nothing." I looked away from him. "I'm fine."

"It's not fine." He guided my head up, so I had to look at him. "What happened? Did Kristina do that?"

Once I told him, he'd want revenge more than he would want to get out of this house.

"Luciana, tell me who hurt you, or I swear on everything holy I will burn this house to the ground with all of them in it."

"Vincent," I whispered.

He squeezed his eyes shut.

"I hit him first."

"That helps." He opened his eyes. "A little."

"He made me mad, so I hit him."

"He shouldn't have hit you back." He took a calming breath. "He's going to die for that."

"That doesn't matter now. They'll kill you if they find you." I panicked. "How did you even get in here?"

"I have my ways." He smirked. "But if we're going to get out the way I came, we have to go now."

"I know this house." I took his hand. "There are guards everywhere."

"There's an old wine cellar at the far end of the property. It's connected to the house by a tunnel. I have men waiting for us on the other side."

"I know the tunnel."

"You do?"

"I had a very lonely childhood, remember?" I often explored the house and the property to get away from my aunt. "I told you I know this house, but how do you?"

"Gio and I researched this place before the engagement party. We gained access to the original owners' blueprints."

"That's how you knew where my bedroom was?"

"I'm the one who put the keys in your room for our new house."

"I always wondered how that package got there."

"You're a sound sleeper." He stroked my cheek. "I sat on the edge of the bed and watched you sleep."

"That's stalkerish."

"Would you expect anything less from me?"

"No." I laughed. "I should be mad."

"I'm sure there are plenty of other things I've done for you to be mad about."

"True."

"You were peaceful, and I told myself I should walk away and leave you alone, but I couldn't do it. I wanted to marry you. I needed you to be mine."

"I'm glad you didn't walk away, but I know how much this alliance has cost you. How much my family has taken from you."

"They've given me much more than they've taken." He took my chin between his fingers. "They gave me you. I'll never regret entering this alliance."

"Even if it gets you killed?" I tried to hold back the tears, but when I thought about the things Vincent said, I couldn't stop myself. "They took me to lure you here. They said they could kill you and the other families wouldn't retaliate because you came into their territory and attacked them."

"None of that matters, Lu." He wiped my tears away. "My only goal is to get you out of here safely and away from them."

"You can't sacrifice yourself for my safety."

"Yeah, I can if it comes to that, but if we go now, we can get out of here undetected." He took my hand and led me down the hall. "I'll deal with them another day."

He looked down at my feet. "Where are your shoes?"

"I don't know. They drugged me and when I woke up, they were gone."

"They drugged you." He tightened his hold on my hand. "I'll show them no mercy."

As we continued down the hall, the house was quiet and dark. We had to make it to the back staircase and down another hall that led to the door that would take us to the section of the basement where the access tunnel was. No one used that entrance. If we wanted to get to the finished part of the basement where the gym and the game room were, we used the door off the kitchen.

"We're almost there," I whispered. "We just have to get to that hallway."

"I know, baby."

My heart strummed loudly between my ears as we hurried through the last archway, but when we turned the corner, my hopes fell into the pit of my stomach.

Romero let go of my hand and drew his gun, taking aim at the dark figure blocking our path. I took a closer look at the man who could ruin all of this for us.

"Sam." I stepped in between them, giving Sam a chance to draw his gun. "Romero, no."

"Lu!" Romero growled at me.

"It's okay." I held up my hand and slowly turned to face Sam. "I want to leave with my husband."

"I can't let you do that," Sam said.

"You know I don't belong here." I pleaded with my eyes, hoping he would remember all the conversations we had when I was growing up. "They've never wanted me. Please, Sam. We don't have much time. If they find us, they'll kill Romero, and if that happens, they might as well kill me, too."

"Sam, I know you care about her," Romero said. "She trusts you. Please trust her."

Sam shifted his attention back to me, his gun still pointed at Romero, and Romero's finger was still on the trigger of his gun. My body trembled when neither of them spoke.

"I have to go with him, Sam," I said. "Please."

Sam lowered his gun and nodded.

"Thank you." I touched his shoulder. "I won't forget this."

"Neither will I." Romero took my hand and hurried me down the hallway. Once we got to the door, he paused.

"What are you doing?" I pointed to the door. "Let's get out of here."

"You can't ever do that again." He pressed me against the door with his body. "Do you understand?"

"Do what?" I breathed heavily under the intensity of his stare.

"Get between me and a gun." He tangled his fingers in my hair. "Do you know how stupid that was?"

"I got Sam to let us go, didn't I?"

"Luciana!" He tightened his grip on my hair. "Promise me you never do that again."

"Hopefully, I'll never have to," I said. "I can't promise that if I have to protect you, I won't do it again."

"You stubborn woman, I protect you." He let go of my hair and placed his hand on the handle of the door. "Never do that again."

I took his hand and followed him down the back staircase and to the door that would lead us out of here. We'd still have to deal with my family, but Romero could do it on his terms.

"We're almost there," I said.

"If anything goes wrong, you don't hesitate. You know where to go. You run as fast as you can and Gio will be on the other side of the tunnel. He'll get you out of here."

"We're going together." I squeezed his hand. "Where you go, I go."

We picked up our pace when the door was in sight. Once we reached it, Romero pulled it open. The familiar smell of the old, wet, damp basement assaulted my nostrils. I could swear the same cobwebs were there when I was a kid. I had forgotten the adventures I used to have exploring the old section of the house and how excited I was when I would make my way out into the beautiful wooded area of the yard. We were almost there. All we had to do was open the heavy oak door and freedom was on the other side.

"I'm impressed." Vincent grabbed my arm. "I didn't even know you knew about this place."

Romero shoved Vincent hard against the door, causing my cousin to drop his gun and lose his hold on me. As Romero moved me out of the way, Vincent got to his feet and swung, hitting Romero's face. Romero retaliated with a hard right hook to Vincent's jaw.

"Lu, go!" Romero yelled, his voice echoing throughout the abandoned part of the house.

As I ran toward the door, the two of them continued to hit one another. I caught a glimpse of Vincent's shiny black gun. It had fallen behind a large steel beam. Romero hadn't removed his gun from the back of his pants because Vincent caught him off guard, and now the two of them were beating the hell out of each other.

Romero wanted me to leave him, but how could I abandon him? He would never leave me. I dropped to my knees and reached for the gun. I inched as close as I could. It was almost in my grasp. I stretched my arm as far as it would go. Just as I retrieved it, Vincent hauled back his fist, but Romero caught it in his hand and pushed him back, causing Vincent to slam into the door and fall to the ground.

"Romero," I yelled.

He turned to find the gun in my shaky hands.

"I thought I told you to go." He moved closer to me and took the gun from me. "Give me that."

I stood behind Romero as he pointed the gun at Vincent, who was too dazed to stand. I dry heaved and my stomach churned at the thought of what would happen next. I remembered how easy it was for Romero to kill those men in the woods. They had done far less to him than my cousin had done. Could I watch as he killed the boy I had grown up with? The man who I called family?

I hated this life and what it had turned them into. Vincent, Rocco, Sandro, Romero, and Gio. They were all better than this. Their fathers made them the men they were. When would it end?

"You're going to pay for what you did to my wife," Romero said. "All of you are."

"No," I whispered so low that Romero didn't even hear me.

"I'd rethink your choices right now, Bilotti," my uncle said from behind us.

We turned to find him, Rocco and three guards all standing with their guns drawn and pointed at us. My aunt stood on the stairs, smiling at me.

We were so close to getting out of here.

CHAPTER 28

Romero

Fuck! If it were just me, I would have taken my chances and shot someone. It wasn't just me though. I could never sacrifice Luciana. Antonio and Rocco held their guns on me, and the three guards aimed theirs at my wife.

"Drop your gun, Bilotti," Rocco said. "There's no way out of this."

He was right. If I fired, they would fire back, and they would catch Luciana in the middle. So, I did the only thing I could, and set the gun on the concrete floor. Vincent quickly retrieved it before getting to his feet and joining his family. I reached for Luciana's hand and tugged her to my side. She stood so close to me that her trembling form practically shook me.

"It's going to be okay." I squeezed her hand. "I promise."

"Don't lie to her," Vincent said. "That's the last memory she'll have of you."

"Why don't we stop playing this game and tell me what the hell you people want from me?" I spoke to Antonio. "You're still running this organization, aren't you?"

"You've always had way too much confidence." He moved closer to us. "You're very much like your father."

"Some would disagree." I glanced at the three men still aiming their guns in this direction. "Why don't you have them stand down? There's no reason to have them aim at Luciana."

As far as everyone thought, I was unarmed. It was Vincent's gun that I had dropped to the floor. Not mine.

"Take your arm off my niece," he said.

They switched their focus to me. Even if I reached for my gun, one of the six would hit me before I could pull the trigger.

"Uncle Antonio," Luciana said. "I've done everything you've asked of me. Please, let us leave."

"I didn't ask you to fall in love with him, did I?" Antonio shook his head in disapproval. "I don't remember asking you to betray your family."

"I made her do that," I said. "The same way you made her betray me. She didn't have a choice."

"She has one now." Antonio looked at Lu. "I'll let your husband go."

"You will?" Lu believed him, but I knew there was a catch.

"All you have to do is agree to stay here with us. Take your rightful place as a Torrio." He smirked. "We'll have this marriage annulled and you can forget the Bilottis ever existed."

"I would do that in a heartbeat," Luciana said.

To protect me.

"But I'm not as naïve as I was before I became a Bilotti." She inched closer to me. "You're not going to spare Romero. That was never the plan. You've always wanted to hurt him and you used me to do it."

"Oh, please." Kristina finally opened her ugly mouth. What the hell was my father thinking when he slept with her? My mother was eloquent, educated, and classy. How could he betray her with Kristina? "You have played the victim in this scenario for far too long. I've waited years for you to stand up and find your voice in this house, but you're not capable of it. The first chance you got, you betrayed us. You're a spineless whore."

"Watch it." When I stepped forward, Rocco stood between me and his mother. My fingers twitched to grab my gun. "I'm growing tired of this. Tell me what this was all for."

"You should never have come back to America," Antonio said. "I've been building an empire for my children. No one has challenged me in years. Not even Dante Marchelli and he has five capable sons who could take over all of this territory, but he stays to himself and only intervenes when he has to."

"What do the Marchellis have to do with this?" I asked.

"That's part of your problem, Romero. You're impatient and impulsive. My point is, the strongest rival family wouldn't challenge me, but you are different."

"I never came after you."

"Not yet," he said. "You would have if given the right opportunity."

"If you would have left me alone, I wouldn't have bothered you as long as we worked peacefully to get my product through the ports. You didn't let that happen, though. You sought me out and propositioned me. I'll admit, I acted hastily and I let a trusted advisor sway me when I should have figured out sooner that he was working for you and not for me."

"Giancarlo?" Antonio laughed. "I have a feeling he won't be seeing another day."

I didn't confirm or deny Antonio's suspicions.

"When you came back to the states, I watched as you became a stronger entity. You gained the respect of the other families quicker than I liked. They couldn't stop talking about you and Gio. How fearless the two of you were. How you were on your way to becoming something bigger than any of us had seen in years."

"They bruised your ego, so you came after me?"

"I had to put a stop to your rein before it got started. My sons will own the streets of New York. The Torrios, not the Bilottis."

"We could have coexisted," I said. "Gio and I never wanted to rule. We're content with our business. If I didn't need you to move product, we never would have crossed paths."

"I don't believe that to be true." Antonio lowered his gun. "Eventually, you would have come after me. It's in your blood. It's who you are. I'm a proactive leader, but the other families would never have let me eliminate you out of respect for your father. I had to create that alliance. I had to bring you down and show them who you really are."

"You took out our warehouse," Vincent said. "Now, you're on our territory trying to take Luciana, who doesn't want to be with you."

"That's not true," Lu shouted. "No one will believe that story because I won't let them."

"Shut up, you little bitch," Kristina said. "Once Romero is out of the picture, I'm going to move to have you put in a mental hospital. We'll say you're not stable. Your husband abused you so badly that you can longer function in society and you need serious help."

I observed Antonio as his wife spoke about his niece.

"I never wanted you here," Kristina continued. "I'm finally getting rid of you."

"What kind of man allows a woman to speak of his sister's child that way?" I asked. "How could you disrespect Stefania's memory like that?"

"What?" Antonio didn't seem as confident as he was a few minutes ago. "You don't know anything about her or our past."

"Let's just say Giancarlo was quite chatty this afternoon and gave me a history lesson on the extracurricular activities of your wife and my father."

"Don't," Kristina said.

"Don't what?" I smirked. "Don't you want your sons to know what kind of woman you really are? Who their mother is?"

"What are you talking about?" Vincent asked.

"Have everyone stand down," I said to Antonio. "The leverage I have against your family will not stay buried if Luciana and I don't walk out of here."

Maybe he didn't care if I exposed his wife's affair, but he would care if I connected her to a murder my father covered up. It would raise all sorts of questions to the other families about who took down my father without permission.

"Lower your guns," Antonio ordered.

"Dad?" Vincent said.

"Don't defy me," Antonio shouted. "Stand down."

The three guards, Rocco, and Vincent all did as Antonio told them to do.

"That's better." I released Lu's hand. "Go to the door."

"What?" She held up her hand. "I'm leaving without you."

"I want you by the door." I motioned toward it. "Go." She wouldn't leave me, but if the shooting started, she'd have a better chance of getting to Gio if she were closer to the tunnel. "Remember what I said earlier. No hesitation."

She closed her eyes and nodded before moving to the door.

"Someone in my organization has a letter with a police file and an autopsy report," I informed Antonio. "If you want to go through with your initial plan of killing me, go for it, but your family will not get out unscathed."

"He's bluffing," Vincent said. "Shoot him."

"No," Lu screamed.

"What is it you think you have?" Rocco said. "If this has to do with your father, that's ancient history. No one cares who took him out. They're probably long gone."

"I don't think they are," I glanced at Antonio. "What do you think?"

"I think you're bluffing," Antonio said. "Whatever Giancarlo told you was probably a lie. He betrayed you once. What makes you think he didn't do it again?"

"Are you really going to make me do this?" I asked. "In front of your sons?"

"What do you think you have, Bilotti?" Rocco yelled. "This is getting old."

"Why don't you ask your mother, Rocco?" I smiled at Kristina. "Maybe she'll finally tell you why she hates your cousin so much. Didn't you ever wonder what would drive her to treat an innocent little girl the way she did?"

"Stop it," Kristina said. "You don't know anything."

"Do you know when she negotiated the terms of the marriage between me and Lu, she hated Luciana so much that she told me if I raped her on our wedding night, no one would blame me?" I wanted to kill Kristina when I thought about that horrible conversation. "She said if Luciana didn't willingly give me her virginity that I should force her."

"Mom?" Rocco gasped.

"She also told me how defiant Lu could be. How spoiled she was." I motioned toward Luciana, who didn't seem at all surprised by any of this. "I learned quickly that the picture your mother painted wasn't correct at all. But, none the less, she said she knew how cruel I could be, and that if I had to beat or torture her to keep her in line, I'd be well within my rights."

"Kristina," Antonio said. "Is this true?"

"Don't act like you care all of a sudden," Kristina pointed at her husband. "You never had the time of day for her. You moved her into this house without consulting me and expected me to take her in as our own."

"My sister was killed in a tragic accident. Stefania was your best friend. Why wouldn't I think you would want to raise Lu as your own?"

"My mother was your best friend?" Luciana asked.

"A long time ago." Kristina pressed her lips together. "She proved to be just as disloyal and weak as you are. She was supposed to have my back, but instead, she caved and tried to betray me the first chance she got." Kristina walked between Rocco and Vincent, but I kept a close eye on her. "She wanted to destroy this family and I would never let that happen. I stopped her before she could."

"What did you do to her?" Luciana asked. "How did you stop her?"

"Why don't you tell her, Kristina?" It looked like that evil witch was going to blow this family up all on her own. "We'd all like to know."

Kristina looked to Antonio for assistance, but he didn't say anything.

"Kill them," she shouted. "Both of them, Antonio. Prove your loyalty to this family."

"All I've ever done is prove my loyalty to this family," he yelled. "If Giancarlo exposed you to Romero, and he has something on you, that's on you. I've protected you long enough."

"What are you saying?" She stepped toward her husband. "I've stood by your side all these years. I've out lasted your affairs and watched you groom our children into mobsters. I let you take control and treat me like an afterthought. Don't you dare act like you did any of this for me."

"Do you really think this is the time to hash this out?" Vincent asked. "We have other pressing matters."

"Vincent is right," Kristina said. "We have to put an end to this."

"No!" Antonio yelled. "How dare you say I've done nothing to protect you." He grabbed her arm and pulled her toward him. "You don't think I know what you did to my sister and her husband? Did you honestly believe I didn't know that you and Bilotti conspired to have them murdered and then covered it up to make it look like an accident?"

"What?" Luciana placed her hand over her mouth.

"You knew?" Kristina whispered.

"I know a lot more than you think." Antonio shook her. "I know exactly who you are."

"Dad, let go of her," Vincent said.

"Shut up." He raised his hand and pushed Vincent away.

"Do you think I'm stupid?" Antonio shouted. "Do you think I believed you went through all of that trouble to cover up an old affair? Did you think I didn't figure out what you were really hiding?"

"Stop this conversation." Kristina shook her head. "Before we all regret it."

"Why?" Antonio asked. "Romero's right. You don't want our sons to know what kind of woman you really are? How you betrayed me in the worst way and violated our vows. You want to throw my indiscretions in my face, but let's be honest. I never cheated on you until after you slept with Mario. You may have ended that affair, but you continued to lie to me for years after. You're still lying to me."

Fuck, all I wanted was leverage to get out of here and get Lu to safety, but even I wanted to know what secret Kristina was hiding.

"It was a mistake." Kristina pushed her hair from her face. "I ended it years ago, but it ate away at me. I confided in Stefania and she wouldn't keep my confidence. She threatened to tell you. That's where she was headed the night of the accident."

"The night someone shot her and Lu's dad in the back of the head and made it look like an accident," I said. "You must have told Stefania about more than just an affair."

"You did that?" Rocco asked.

"I didn't have a choice," she said. "I had to protect this family."

"What did you tell her?" Luciana said. "What did my parents lose their lives for? I deserve to know how I ended up here to endure your torment."

"If you don't tell her," I said. "I'll keep digging. I'll make sure Luciana knows the full truth. If Antonio figured it out, I'm sure I can too."

"I'll save you the trouble," Antonio said. "There will be no reason for you to keep digging around in the past."

"Antonio," Kristina pleaded.

"I'm doing this to protect my family," Antonio said. "She had an affair with your father after Vincent was born. It lasted for about a year, but I suspect it may have gone on longer than I knew. They ended it when my wife became pregnant with Rocco."

"No." Kristina paced the room. "None of this should ever have come out."

"So, she ended things when she found out you were going to have a baby." Vincent said. "This is between the two of you. Can we table this conversation and act like the fucking leading mafia family we're supposed to be instead of a goddamn soap opera?"

"Unless." Rocco seemed to have a revelation as he stared at his mother. "She ended things with

Bilotti and came back to you when she realized he got her pregnant."

"Don't be ridiculous," Vincent said. "That would mean you're a Bilotti."

"That's what you confided in Stefania years later," I said. "That's why you can't stand her daughter. She was going to tell her brother your secret. She was going to tell him my father got you pregnant."

"Rocco." Kristina's eyes filled with tears. "It's not true."

"You're lying," Lu said. "That's why you hate my mother."

"You stupid bitch." Kristina grabbed Luciana and then pulled a silver knife from her pocket, pressing it to Lu's throat. "This is all your fault."

I took my gun from my waistband and aimed it at Kristina's head just as Vincent and the three guards pointed their weapons at me.

"Romero," Vincent said. "You're not going to stand a chance."

"Maybe not." I stared into Luciana's eyes, wanting hers to be the last thing I saw before I lost this battle. I could die a happy man knowing she loved me. "But you can bet your ass, I'll blow your mother's head off before any of you pull the trigger."

CHAPTER 29

Luciana

Kristina pressed the blade to my neck with a steady hand. The only thing that helped me breathe was Romero's stunning green eyes. I trusted him with my life, but I didn't want him to lose his defending me.

"Romero, please," I said. "Don't get yourself killed."

My legs buckled when Romero tightened his grip on his gun. I closed my eyes, hoping he would hit me instead, because once he fired, Vincent and the guards would fire back and they would kill my husband. I couldn't imagine my life without him in it.

"Stop." Rocco stepped in between Romero and Vincent, blocking any clean shots from either side.

"What the fuck are you doing?" Vincent asked.
"It's time to end this."

"If any of what was said here is true, Romero is my brother," Rocco said. "I can't let you kill him."

"I'm *your* brother," Vincent yelled. "You are a Torrio even if blood proves otherwise, and you are my brother."

Kristina relaxed her stance, probably distracted over Rocco and Vincent's exchange. I didn't waste the opportunity. I slung my elbow back, nailing her in the stomach. When she fell to the floor, I kicked her in the ribs before retrieving her knife.

"Now, who is the stupid bitch?" I turned to find all the men in the room staring at me in disbelief. Well, not Romero. He was laughing.

I ran and stood next to Rocco, obstructing any shots that could be fired at my husband.

"Lu." Romero yanked my arm and shielded me with his body. "What did I tell you about that?"

"I would do anything to protect you." Why was that so difficult for him to understand?

"This has been quite the shit show," Romero said. "I wasn't bluffing when I said if anything happened to me, that report would be released to the families, launching an investigation into what happened to my father. After listening to your family drama, it's obvious you people might not care what gets released."

"Do you think we're just going to let you walk out of here?" Vincent asked.

"No, but I didn't come alone." Romero's gun was

still raised. "My retrieval of Luciana took a lot longer than I expected and I instructed my men to take no prisoners. If I don't come out of here, my team will blow this place up. We're good at that."

"You don't think our guards are prepared for something like that?" My uncle glanced at my aunt, who pushed herself into a seated position.

"Don't forget, I managed to get in here undetected, but I know how many guards you have on a shift." Romero motioned toward the three who were still holding their guns on us. "They're already down three. I can't guarantee that my men haven't started taking out the ones surrounding the house. Trust me, I brought a fucking army with me and they won't stop until I'm avenged."

"Dad." Rocco closed his eyes, and I heard the pain in his voice when he realized his whole life might be a lie. "Let them go."

"Romero can go," my uncle said. "The alliance is over. Luciana stays here."

"No." When I stepped closer to my uncle, Romero moved with me and everyone else seemed to shift their focus, still keeping their guns raised. "I'm going with my husband. Haven't you kept me a prisoner long enough?"

"You're choosing the Bilottis over your family?"

"I'm a Bilotti." I smiled at Romero. "You made sure of that, and if we're being honest, it's the only good thing you've ever done for me."

"You ungrateful little —"

"Kristina!" My uncle held up his hand. "I'd hold my tongue if I were you. You have a lot of explaining to do to your sons tonight." He looked at Romero. "I underestimated you."

"A lot of people do, but they don't make that mistake twice." Romero nodded to the guards and Vincent. "If I don't get out of this, neither do you and your family."

"This isn't over." My uncle raised his hand. "Lower your weapons. They're leaving."

Rocco let out a breath as Vincent and the guards did what they were told. Romero took my hand in his, still holding his gun. He walked backward, because he wouldn't dare take his eyes off the others as I led us to the door.

"I won't forget what you did," he said to Rocco.

Rocco didn't respond. He had so many demons to deal with. I didn't envy him.

As I opened the old, wooden door, I took pleasure knowing that no matter what happened from this point forward, I would never have to come back into this house ever again. I didn't look back. Once we were outside, Romero held my hand tighter, rushed in front of me, and hurried through the tunnel and into the night air.

I squinted in the light of the bright flashlights when we got to the end.

"What the fuck?" Gio greeted us. "What took so long?"

"We hit a few bumps?" Romero hugged him. "We're good though."

"Nice to see you, beauty." Gio grabbed me and lifted me off my feet. "Don't get kidnapped again."

"I'll try not to." I laughed. "Thanks for rescuing me."

"We need to go." Romero scooped me off my feet.

"What are you doing?" I asked.

"You don't have any shoes on." He carried me toward the waiting SUV. "Your feet must be sore."

"I haven't even thought about it," I said. "I was distracted by the possibility that you were going to get killed, I was going to get my throat slashed, the revelation that Rocco could possibly be your brother, and that they let us go."

"Wait? What?" Gio said. "What was that about Rocco being our brother?"

"It got a little weird in there." Romero shrugged. "It turns out Kristina's affair with dad may have produced another sibling for us."

"I didn't see that coming." Gio opened the car door for us. "That's going to be interesting."

"Yeah, well, that's a problem for another day." Romero lowered me into the backseat and then turned to Gio.

"We have a few things to deal with. The Feds, the

cartel, the other families, apparently a new sibling." Gio gave me a thumbs up. "I look forward to it all."

"We'll see you back at the house. Clear everyone out of here. We have plenty to discuss." He nodded toward the tunnel. "This is not over. They're going to come for us, and when they do, we need to be ready."

"We will be." Gio patted Romero's back. "I'm glad you're both okay."

Romero got into the backseat with me and shut the door. Salvi turned and smiled at us before driving out of the woods and onto a dirt road that would eventually take us off the property.

"My parents." I had so much to process, but none of it had really hit me yet.

"My father had them killed. I wasn't sure why until I found out about Rocco. I'm sorry."

"It's not your fault." I patted his hand because he was going through a lot, too. "We have a lot of issues to sort through."

"We'll do it together."

"I should have listened to you." I rested my head on his shoulder.

"Those are words I like to hear coming out of your mouth." He wrapped his arm around me. "Which part?"

"I shouldn't have gone to brunch."

"You didn't know, but from now on we'll go with my instincts." He kissed the top of my head. "Be prepared, butterfly, I'm never letting you out of my sight. If you thought I was overbearing before, well, it's about to get a lot worse."

"They're not going to leave us alone, are they?" The only reason we walked out of that house was because Kristina's revelation had thrown them all off balance. If Romero didn't have that leverage, they would have killed him and I would have watched him die. "I'm grateful we're together, but we're not safe."

"I'll handle all of that." He held me close. "I'll figure it out."

"Are you proud of me?"

"Always."

"No, I mean, for defending myself and getting away from Kristina and her knife?"

"So, about that." His muscles tensed. "You did good, but you almost gave me a heart attack when you went back to kick her."

"You didn't like that? I thought that was something you would do."

"It's exactly something I would do, but you are not me. Once you escape, you keep running. You should have left out the door like I told you to."

"I couldn't leave you." I kissed his cheek. "I love you."

"I love you too, but when I tell you not to step between me and a gun, or when I tell you to run, I want you to listen to me without hesitation." He pulled me into his lap. "If anything ever happens to you, I'll lose my mind. I can't be without you."

"I feel the same way, Romero." A tear slid down my cheek. "I can't lose you. Don't you understand you're all I have?"

"Don't cry." He wiped my face. "You can't get rid of me."

"Promise?"

"Promise." He pressed my knuckles to his lips. "Tonight, we start the rest of our lives together. It's you and me, baby."

"I wouldn't want it any other way."

He took my face between his hands and kissed me with the possessiveness I expected from him. I was his, and he was mine. When he released me from his hold, I struggled to catch my breath. I rested my head on his chest and took comfort in his firm hold.

As we drove down the dark road, I settled into him. He stroked my hair, twisting the ends around his fingers, calming my restless soul. No matter what waited for us, we would face it together. My husband, my soulmate, my world...

THE END

HIS BROKEN QUEEN

Her decision to choose me has deadly consequences.

The alliance that gave me my bride is over. I couldn't trust her family, and now they have vowed to come after me... after us.

The division among the top mafia families is mounting, as they must choose between two feuding organizations. The conflicts leave us vulnerable to a dangerous enemy. One that could bring us all down. Everything I worked so hard for is in jeopardy, but I have to keep Luciana safe at all costs.

If we run I'll lose everything, but even worse, if we stay I could lose her.

Sacrifices are inevitable, but the wrong decisions could destroy us both.

Will my queen stand beside me, or will she finally cave to the pressure of this savage life, and escape my world once and for all?

Continue with the Sold to The Mafia Boss saga. This dark and addicting series can't be missed. Start at the beginning with *Ruthless Saints* to see how it all begins.

The books in this series should be read in this order:

Ruthless Saints
Her Heartless King
His Broken Queen

ABOUT THE AUTHOR

USA Today Bestselling author Ella Jade has been writing for as long as she can remember. As a child, she often had a notebook and pen with her, and now as an adult, the laptop is never far. The plots and dialogue have always played out in her head, but she never knew what to do with them. That all changed when she discovered the eBook industry. She started penning novels at a rapid pace and now she can't be stopped.

Ella resides in New Jersey with her husband, two boys, and two feisty Chihuahua writing companions. She can often be found creating sexy, domineering men and the strong women who know how to challenge them in and out of the bedroom. She hopes you'll get lost in her words.

Printed in Great Britain
by Amazon